D0638537

A Family Gathering

A Family Gathering

T. Alan Broughton

HR

A Henry Robbins Book

E. P. DUTTON | NEW YORK

Copyright © 1977 by T. Alan Broughton
All rights reserved. Printed in the U.S.A.

No part of this publication may be reproduced or transmitted in any form or by any means, electronic or mechanical, including photocopy, recording, or any information storage and retrieval system now known or to be invented, without permission in writing from the publisher, except by a reviewer who wishes to quote brief passages in connection with a review written for inclusion in a magazine, newspaper, or broadcast.

LIBRARY OF CONGRESS CATALOGING IN PUBLICATION DATA

Broughton, Thomas Alan, 1936–
A family gathering.

"A Henry Robbins book."
I. Title.
PZ4.B874538Fam [PS3552.R68138] 813'.5'4
76-45454

ISBN: 0-525-10310-4

Published simultaneously in Canada by Clarke, Irwin & Company Limited, Toronto and Vancouver

10 9 8 7 6 5 4 3 2 1

First Edition

PS
3552
R68138F3

For My Father

Quo res cumque cadent, unum et commune periclum,
una salus ambobus erit.

Midwest 5.57 clc
12/2/81
428363

A Family Gathering

1

Still dazed with sleep when they turned into the driveway, Lawson sensed the slowing motions of the car and sat up to discover himself in the back seat, Uncle Edward smiling beside him, and his mother and father in front talking excitedly. They passed the gaunt white posts, old gateway of a fence where neither gate nor fence remained, and drove slowly over the loose stone road to the house with its jutting, white-pillared porch. Three dogs ran down the field to meet them and followed barking and snapping beside the wheels. His aunt and uncle were standing on the steps, then Uncle Brody started walking down toward them.

"There they are," his mother said and waved too from the front seat. His father honked the horn, and the dogs swerved away but came back. Lawson covered his ears, distancing all the sounds, and everything floated quietly—his uncle standing with hands on his hips now, smiling as they approached, Aunt

Esther above him on the porch, her arms in a V on her body, her mouth saying something, his father and mother still waving, their talking muffled, and the head of a dog bobbing into sight, tongue hanging out and eyes shyly askance. Edward sat very still and straight, a half-finished smile on his lips, and when he started to speak, Lawson said, "What?" His own voice burst and was smothered in his head. He took away his hands, but it was too late. The car had stopped and Uncle Brody was trying to open the locked door, his round face puffed with red.

"Well, here they are, Esther, here's Jacqueline and Bailey." He quit trying to open the door and leaned partway in the window. "And Lawson, hello, sonny, and here's Edward Ambler too, we thought you'd never get here," and at the same time Bailey and Jacqueline were protesting something and laughing, and Jacqueline unlocked the door so that Brody staggered back with it, then leaned and kissed her flatly on the cheek while Bailey was getting out his side, and Aunt Esther came around the front of the car to meet him halfway where they hugged each other awkwardly for a moment as the dogs leaped and whined and wriggled their backsides. Brody stood back and helped Jacqueline out and took her by the shoulders to kiss her again and by that time Esther had come around and the two women stepped in close to hug with their heads craning over each other's shoulders until Esther pushed away, her hands on Jacqueline's hips and she said, "Why, Jacqueline, you're all skin and bones, I declare you're just a slip of a girl again," and his mother denied it shyly. "Bailey," Esther said over all the other voices, "what have you been doing, starving your family?" but the two brothers were standing in close, pumping each other's hand, and Brody put his free hand down hard with a slap on Bailey's shoulder again and again. Then he turned suddenly to push away the dogs leaping at everyone and nosing the women. "Here," he yelled, "git on with you, git," and he caught the spotted dog with the side of his foot so that it yelped and circled away with a guilty look on its face.

"And Lawson," Aunt Esther squealed when he began to get out of the car. "Why, look at the boy, he's all grown into a young man, come here, sonny, and give your aunt a hug," which he did, being pressed into the full body by her strong hands, which slapped at his back, and he smelled that flowery, furniture-polish odor that he remembered was hers. Then he put out his hand, which Uncle Brody enveloped in his. "Well, well," Brody said, "why you're almost as tall as I am, mighty tall for a twelve-year-old, I'd say," which he thought a terrible exaggeration until he saw that actually his uncle was not much taller—only his bulk made Lawson feel small.

"We were delayed," his father was saying as he opened the trunk of the car. Esther and his mother began to talk their way up to the porch, arms around each other's waist.

"Here, don't you worry about the luggage now, Richard will take care of all that. You remember Richard, don't you? We hired him and some of the boys from town for a week. Richard? Richard," he began to bawl, and around the corner of the house came the figure of a middle-aged Negro smiling and nodding, and he was wearing a white linen jacket.

"Here, now," and Brody standing between his father and Lawson slapped them both on the back, pushing them firmly away from the car. "Let's get in so we can have a drink before dinner. Richard'll take care of all this. Richard, you can just put all these things in the hall, we'll sort them later."

That was when Edward's legs unfolded from the back door of the car. Brody stopped. "Lord, Edward Ambler, I was so excited I forgot," and as if to make up for it he came at the man with both his hands out. "Esther," he yelled, "Esther, here's Edward been forgot in all the excitement. Why, you must think us the worst sort of hosts. Esther," he bawled again and his wife shrieked.

"Not at all, not at all," Edward was saying as they surrounded him. Finally he raised a flattened palm and closed his eyes. "I won't hear another word."

“All right, all right,” Brody said and they all began walking up to the porch again.

“I don’t think I’ve been out this way for some years,” Edward continued in that precise and slow manner that usually annoyed Lawson, especially when he was telling a story at the dinner table, but that now seemed calming. “I was in Lynchburg four years back, I believe, but I can’t recall leaving Richmond more than once or twice since, and that was only to visit.”

“Well,” Brody said as if uncertain what to do with the information.

The dogs had calmed down and began to wander around, sniffing at the luggage Richard was pulling out of the car, and one of them lifted a leg but Richard caught him in time, and then they went off toward the big oak where they circled and flopped down in the grass. “And you’ve been well?” Brody said as they approached the porch.

Uncle Edward paused, hands behind his back and head turned slightly to the side as if listening to something inside himself. “I’ve managed,” and his fingers clenched and unfurled like a heartbeat.

When they started up the steps his father glanced quickly over his shoulder as if someone were following too closely, and Brody was telling something about the barn. Then old Emily, the cook, and her husband, James, who always worked around the house, came out and said hello and how nice it was to see them back home again, and when they came to Lawson, once more he was told how much he had grown. He lagged behind on the lawn. The long sleep, the noisy waking, made him alert. There was a smell of new grass, of the lilac bushes by the porch, and he could see down across the lawn and the field to the woods and river. Bright patches of dandelions broke yellow from the ground. He felt as though he were waking up after the passing of a heavy thunderstorm. So many things to do, places to go. They were all talking at once on the porch, except for Edward, but even he was nodding politely to Brody who was pointing and explaining something. Lawson had been told by his mother that because of the preparations for the wedding, not much attention would be paid to him, and he would have to be a good boy, take care of himself, and stay out of the way for a few days. But that was what he wanted anyway. Richard passed him with arms full of luggage. They grinned at each other. From the front steps he could see over and down the long slope to the barn and beyond to Fletcher Hill and the rolling lowlands. There were long dirt roads back there, cabins and farms and fallen-down places where no one lived anymore. There were secret things to see and do. Brody had come down a step. He was laughing and put his hand on Lawson's shoulder, kneading it.

The luggage was sorted. Lawson was to sleep in the same room with Uncle Edward. "You don't mind, do you?" Edward said politely after his parents had gone to their room and the two of them were left alone together to unpack. They were told to hurry because dinner was ready and Uncle Brody was still eager for a drink.

"Nope, I don't," although at the moment they were left together Lawson was not sure. He had never slept in the same room with anyone else. But Edward was his favorite uncle, even if he was a little odd. Besides, he wasn't a Wright since he was his mother's brother, and Lawson had promised his mother that he would show Edward around and help him feel at home.

"I believe I'll take the bed by the door, if you don't mind," he said slowly, and Lawson watched him look carefully at the bed and then the door as if measuring the distance between them. But he was used to his uncle's quirks and had long ago learned how harmless they were.

His parents came to get him. As they went downstairs, Brody called to them, "Out here, on the porch," where he stood by a tray full of cold drinks on a table. Aunt Esther plucked up two and gave them to Bailey and Jacqueline.

"What'd you bring for sonny here, Esther?"

Lawson was hanging back slightly. His mother had fussed at his hair all the way down the stairs and he was still scowling. He hated the way women pestered around.

"Do you like lemonade?" she reached out a tall glass to him and Lawson took it.

"Yes, ma'm."

"It's long past time the boy had a taste of good bourbon, isn't it, Bailey?" and Brody shook his glass so the ice cubes clinked. "Remember how Grampa used to let us each take a sip of his before dinner? Why, I was only six then." He put a hand on his hip where the belt of his slacks creased out a fold of flesh. "Here now, sit down, sit down."

"It's been such a cool spring," Esther was saying, "that we haven't had the time to enjoy being outside in the evening. This is almost the first time."

They sat in the wicker chairs around the table, but Lawson went to the swinging divan, making the old chains squeak as he set them in motion. The rasp of the swing reminded him of those hot afternoons in the summers when they had come to stay before, sometimes so hot that the only breeze was the breeze of his motion as he swung, or of the evening, fireflies lighting up on the lawn and sometimes drifting in to land on the cushions and glow purple. He sipped his lemonade slowly. It was a little sour but he decided not to ask for some sugar since he wanted to be left alone. After his father and Brody had another drink, Edward came down and had some tea. The thin shadow of a cloud floated over the distant woods and up the long field until it reached them and for a moment the dandelions turned brownish, the grass gray, and a gust of chill wind sent a pile of napkins flying. By the time the two brothers and Edward had retrieved them, the cloud was past, the wind gone, and a small red convertible was spinning up the driveway to the house, opening a fan of dust behind it.

His cousin Bonnie was sitting up on top of the back seat, a

boy below on either side of her like the escorts of a queen on a float. Up front were three girls, all in bright-colored bathing suits and hats and bandannas, but most of their tanned flesh showed. The car stopped. One of the boys pushed on the back door with his foot and gave Bonnie his hand to hold onto as she clambered over him. She was dressed in a scant, two-piece bathing suit, a large straw hat on her head. They handed her a mesh bag when she was out and standing tiptoed on the gravel.

"Hi, Mr. Wright," the driver said and gave a lazy wave. She stared flatly at each of the strangers on the porch, and when she looked at him, Lawson stared back.

Brody called out, "Hello, Nora," and then in sotto voce to the others said, "Nora Smith, maid of honor."

"Hello, Nora," and Esther stood.

"Why, hello, Miz Wright. I didn't see you there." She waved again, racing the engine softly, said, "Bye now," and they were off again, Nora driving with one hand and holding her hat with the other, and the boys had their faces turned to the porch with the same blank curiosity they had shown since arriving. One of them lifted a casual hand from the back of the seat to Bonnie who stood facing them, and like a fish raising one fin before diving, the car turned its back and rolled off past the field.

Bonnie turned up the path, her bag over one slim shoulder, as though walking itself were a pleasure and she didn't mind showing it.

"Uncle Bailey, Aunt Jacqueline," she piped as she came up the steps, and she stood on tiptoes to Bailey, almost touching against him, then kissed him on the cheek. She hugged her aunt.

"My," Jacqueline said when they parted, "you are a beautiful sight."

"Oh," and for the first time her poise was shaken as though her own thoughts had been discovered.

"You remember my brother, Edward, don't you?"

Edward was standing, smiling, his teacup clasped in both hands.

"Of course. How are you?"

"I am very well, thank you," he was saying but before he could finish Brody said, "and here's your cousin, Lawson."

She turned. Lawson stood up from the swing, which came back and nudged him gently on his thighs.

"Lawson? For heaven's sake. Give me a hug."

She came to him, both her arms out, and he stepped into them shyly, almost as tall as she was, and as her arms went around him, he smelled the sunoil on her neck and touched her bare back lightly with his hands. Quick as a squirrel she was away again, one hand holding him by the arm.

"He's grown."

"Who were those awful boys?" her mother said.

"They're friends of Nora, staying with her. Besides, they're not awful."

"Well, they need a lesson in manners, dear."

When she came down later she was dressed simply, her hair gathered in a tight knot. They had already begun dinner. As soon as Bonnie arrived, the conversation turned to her wedding. The two brothers teased her and she led them on. They all laughed at some of the things she said, but when they did she was not angry and laughed too. Lawson remained very quiet except when he was addressed. He began to see that getting married was something very special, but sometimes he was embarrassed for her and wondered how she could stand all that kidding without getting angry. He was sitting beside her and found her very easy to talk with, even though he had not seen her for three years. She seemed much more friendly than she used to be and wanted to know everything about his school. He told her as much as he could.

"I bet the girls like you now," she said finally.

He scowled. "Nope."

"Oh, come on."

They were silent for a minute.

"I tell you what. Tomorrow you've got to help me keep busy, all right? We'll go on a picnic or something. The wedding's so soon and I'll be nervous, and my friends don't help because they just keep teasing me, so you and I, we'll figure something to do."

Lawson thought he liked the idea, although if the suggestion had come from his mother or aunt he would have groaned aloud. Even if she was a cousin, she was a girl.

After dinner they went out to the porch, but Bonnie and her mother stayed and when the others were outside they could hear them arguing, their words not clear but the tone definite. Esther was being very firm and Bonnie's voice worked around hers. After a while Esther came out alone. The others had sat down again except for Edward who stood on the edge of the porch, hands in his pockets, looking down over the fields. Lawson sat on the bottom step and patted the dog lying there on its side. He looked over at Edward who was half-hidden by a trellis, a mild, almost sad look on the man's face. He seemed to follow the distant figure of a running dog for a while and then he was not looking at anything in particular, eyes unfocused. Lawson wanted to say something to him, but he could think of nothing so he turned and began digging at the corner of one flagstone with the toe of his shoe where a group of small, red ants were scurrying and bumping in the dirt.

After a while she came out, freshly powdered and perfumed, in the same dress but carrying a sweater over one arm. The sky was beginning to darken, and down across the field single trees merged into the blot of forest. The porch was already dusky.

"Now, Bonnie, you be back before midnight, you hear?"

"Oh, mother."

"I mean it."

"Yes, mother."

Then Esther put her arms around Bonnie until she touched her head carefully against her mother's shoulder while they rocked gently back and forth.

"Bonnie, what ever am I going to do without my baby to scold anymore?"

"Mama," Bonnie said softly and everyone was very still, only the swing sighing gently back and forth.

Bonnie came lightly down the steps to where Lawson was sitting. She reached down and took his hand and made him stand, then broke a small blossom off the lilac bush and stuck it in her hair.

"Come on, let's go for a walk. They won't be here for a while."

She started down the lawn toward the oak tree and he followed. "My mother scolds at me all the time like that. Does yours?"

"Sometimes."

"You know, I think it's the hardest thing in the world being an only child, don't you? I just wish I had an older brother."

Lawson had thought of that often. His friend George had three sisters, and he seemed to get away with everything.

"You wait till you start going out nights, and all. Except I suppose it's always easier for men."

Lawson was ashamed that he was not older and had not yet begun to go out at night, but at the same time he didn't think he ever would. He would not know what to do.

"Of course, if mama only knew," she said in a whisper and then she took the flower out of her hair and threw it into the air. They reached the wide spread of the tree, the leaves of the bottom branches just over their heads. Lawson did not ask her what she meant because she seemed to be talking to herself.

"I love this old tree. I used to climb it when I was a little girl. Remember that time you and your parents came about seven years ago? 'Course, I don't expect you could. That was one of the first times you came." She plucked down a leaf and began weaving the stalk into its fan. "You were only four or five then and I was eleven and just a little girl. You used to watch me climb and you thought it was the funniest thing. I'd get up in a branch and hang by my legs and you'd stand here and laugh and laugh. Don't you remember at all?"

They went in under the branches and she sat down on the grass. Lawson hesitated for a moment, then sat too.

"I do, sort of."

"Now, here I am about to be married."

The grass was very cool, although not damp yet. For a while the lawn had a grayish light to it and then even that was gone. The tree stirred lightly in a breeze as though darkness were washing in, a small, high-reaching wave of wind that flowed up the long field to the crest of the hill. They were silent for some time. The voices of the adults were brought to them on a gust making them seem very close, and then they could not be heard again except for occasional bursts of laughter, mostly Aunt Esther's.

"What shall we do tomorrow? Do you like to swim?"

"Uh-huh."

"I know the nicest place where we can go. We'll take a lunch. I hope it'll be a good day."

"So do I."

Then she put her hand on his arm, gripping it tightly. "There's so much I want to tell you. I declare I've got to talk to somebody about all this. You'll let me talk to you, won't you?"

She leaned close and spoke so tensely that he could not answer. Headlights burned into the field below and began winding toward them.

"Here they come. I'll have to run now. Good night, Lawson. See you tomorrow, hear?" and she leaned over, took his head between her cool hands and kissed him on his mouth.

He saw her for a moment as a gray blur of motion, then only heard her running through the grass, and finally that was covered by the rumble of the coming car until she was silhouetted by their headlights and the car stopped for her. As though to avoid going all the way up the hill to the house, it turned there, shifting and reversing a few times, and finally the wheels spun and the headlights lit the side of the road so quickly that it seemed to be moving too. Lawson reached up and grasped the end of the branch over his head.

At first he thought he was angry, but he could not decide what to be angry at. They were laughing on the porch. But it was too dark for them to see him, so they couldn't be making fun of him. But his mother would call him soon or he would go back and Uncle Brody would make some joke at him. Then he was angry at her. When he felt how flushed his cheeks were, he wanted to hit himself and instead stripped the leaves from the branch and balled them in his hand. She was only his cousin, and what was she doing kissing him like that? He opened his fist and rolled the crushed leaves between his hands and then smelled the green on them.

"Lawson. Law-son?"

His mother. He did not answer for a moment.

"Yoo-hoo?"

He began walking toward the house. "I'm coming."

"Where were you?" his father's voice came from the dark above. They had not turned on any porch lights and the bowl of Brody's pipe glowed red.

"Just walking."

"It's almost time for your bed, young man," his mother's voice said, but even though he tried to sound angry when he said, "Oh," he really did not mind. He wanted to be by himself.

Esther seemed to be somewhere just behind them. "You know, Jacqueline, I'm so glad you can stay on a little after the wedding. It'll be so much fun. And Lawson will love it. We can find someone here for him to play with, I'm sure."

"Yes . . ." Jacqueline began.

"No, really," and Brody's pipe cut an arc on the air as he gestured. "I think it's about time you took a little time off to relax, Bailey. Especially now there's no hurry to get back. It's going to be like old times. Plenty to do here for a while. It feels so right to have you back."

All evening Bailey had been waiting for something to rub against his nerves and was surprised at how relaxed he continued to be. Now, even though he did not feel thankful, he said, "Thank you," simply, and thought that he found it typical of his brother to remind him so bluntly of the one fact, the loss of his job, that he wanted to bury in the back of his mind, and had buried in a strange euphoria since driving across the flatlands that afternoon from Richmond, watching the road he knew so well unroll like a black, curving carpet into the foothills of the Blue Ridge, leading them at last to the winding driveway and the house. He didn't like Brody's tone of voice, the implication that he knew what was best for his younger brother. A little rest. Only an oblique intimation of what Bailey knew was on all their minds, how he had been acting odd lately. Well, he didn't want to be absorbed by their concern, thank you, by Brody's incessant "family spirit." For three years Bailey had refused with polite excuses to "come home," as Brody insisted on calling it, and now all the old doubts and irritations were washing in again. But he swirled his brandy and controlled himself, knowing he was tired, and Brody certainly meant well. Always, he meant well.

"Well, it's just grand," and again Brody's pipe struck out like a falling star.

They all stopped talking. One of the dogs was barking and a man's voice came to them from the driveway.

"Quiet, boy," he was saying to the dog.

Esther called out, "Is that you, Charlie?"

"Yes, ma'm."

"Why, here's Charlie Hutter."

The porch lights went on, revealing Brody by the switch and the others leaning forward and blinking in the bright light. Edward was standing against one of the porch pillars with his back to everyone. Bailey saw he had a telescope in his hand, the old brass one his father had used and that they still kept on the mantel. At the bottom of the steps stood a thin, young man, wearing a white shirt open at the neck. The dogs whined and wagged their tails, thrusting their noses at his hands, but he pushed them away.

"Charlie, I'm so glad you dropped by," Esther said.

"Bonnie isn't about, is she?"

"No. I thought you'd be with her."

He had a shy smile and when he talked his eyes shifted quickly from face to face as though afraid of staring too long in any one place.

"No, ma'm. It's bad luck to be with the bride for a week before the wedding. I was pretty sure she was going out tonight, but I was afraid she might have stayed home."

But his voice sounded a little disappointed. Brody came down to him and took his elbow, urging him up. "A week? That's longer than I've heard say, old man. You're not really that superstitious, are you? Meet the folks."

"Actually it was my grandmother said so. She made Bonnie promise. Evening, Miz Wright," and he reached out for Esther's hand.

"Charlie, now when are you going to call me 'mother'?"

"I don't know, ma'm. I've called you Miz Wright for so long, I'm not sure I can change over," and he put his hands on his hips as though he were uncertain what to do with them.

To each one he muttered a "how-do-you-do" and shook hands. He had a wiry grip, quickly given and withdrawn. His upper teeth protruded slightly and his smile showed that he knew.

"I've been looking at the stars," Edward said as if he felt the need to explain himself, but no one replied.

"Sit down, Charlie," and Brody brought up a chair that had been back against the wall.

"No, sir, thank you. I was just out walking and I thought I

could hear voices so I stopped by because I remembered Bonnie saying you-all were coming today."

Esther began to move to the door. "Well, sit, sit. Can I get you a beer?"

"Oh, no, ma'm. Really."

He started toward the stairs. "Besides I wouldn't want to be here if Bonnie came home," and he looked at Esther as though he hoped for some reply, but when none came he made an awkward bow from the top of the stairs. "Well, I'm pleased to have met you folks. Bonnie, she told me about you often."

They all admitted it had been a pleasure, the dogs came up out of the dark again, then with a wave he joined them and disappeared over the lawn. For a while everyone was silent.

"Nice looking young man," Bailey said because he knew something had to be said.

"Good honest boy," Brody answered abruptly as though he had saved up something to say, and Esther's voice flowed in quickly, "We're so glad for Bonnie. When I think of the other ones she might have chosen. And he is a local boy, you know, and it means she shan't be all that far from home." A deep breath, and then her voice trembled slightly. "It's hard when there's only one child."

"Well, now, Esther, you don't have to tell Bailey and Jacqueline about that, I guess. They'll see when it comes time for Lawson to marry." Brody laughed. "Got your girl picked out, Lawson?"

Bailey tried to think of a way to interrupt. He could see his son staring out past Edward into the dark, and he did not want the boy to say something rude. But he wouldn't blame him. Lately, especially when he felt the distance growing between himself and Jacqueline, he found it hard to look at his son without a sharp tug, then a need to touch him. Partly, he knew, this was a common state of mind for a father to be in, especially when he saw a puzzled look on the boy's face and remembered what it was like to be that age, how everything was beginning to flow in and skin seemed sensitive to it all, but none of it made sense yet. If it ever did. That was just part of watching your child grow up. But at other times he saw himself as about to hurt his boy in some way he did not know yet, even though he didn't want that to happen. One afternoon recently he had been sitting in his study, staring out the window that squared off the backyard—the same tree, same garden, same paths, and he was tired of them. When he turned Lawson was standing in the doorway, staring at him blankly, as if he were a window also. That made him nervous. "Can't you see I'm trying to work?" he said sharply, and Lawson frowned, stepped without a word from the doorway, and Bailey turned back to the window, his eyes closed.

"Well, he's the only male Wright in his generation," Brody was saying since no one had answered him. "So that'll be some wedding."

Again there was a long pause. The moon had begun to appear and a single moth was beating up against the porch light. What was it in the moth, the light, the summer air full of lilacs that made Bailey recall something? He wanted the porch to himself for a while. It was always this way when he first came back to the house that he and Brody had grown up in. So many memories were lurking in objects, even sounds or smells, but if he did not let them open out in the first few days, they would sink back again, lost somewhere until the next time. He yawned. So that was the bridegroom, Charlie Hutter. He glanced at Jacqueline talking so easily with Esther and Brody, at Lawson almost dozing now, and what he had felt for months came back, an edginess that only increased at night, not making him turn in bed but lie awake and stare at the ceiling, and he would pretend sleep, not wanting to talk to Jacqueline about the way he felt or to make excuses. Sometimes he seemed to wake and doze without being able to tell the difference. During the day he was nervous, smoked too much, found himself sweating profusely at times for no apparent reason.

Edward put the telescope to his eye as if something had come into sight, but then he let his hands drop slowly, and he shook his head. Of course Edward was the unstable one, and they expected him to be, but Bailey knew that lately Jacqueline was worried about him also. He envied the way Edward was shielded, his eccentricities expected and harmless. But what scared Bailey was that his lapses might become dangerous, not just to himself but to the others around him. Driving that afternoon he had seen them all go to sleep, one by one, until he was the only one awake, steering them through the pale colors of the early summer countryside where groves of cherry trees bleached the fields beyond the red banks of the road. There was an odd sense of hazard, whether it was crows that lifted ponderously out of the middle of the road to slant away to the fields or swallows that flicked across from the banks but always swerved and rode up at the last moment as though the car pushed a gentle shield of air in front of it. Bailey had wondered how they could tell the car was coming, although in places along the road there were small gray lumps, a ragged wing thrust up. He did not start or swerve when the birds flecked the corner of his eye. If they could not avoid him, there was nothing he could do, but when he hit one his hands trembled for a long time afterward.

Then he pulled out beside a heavy truck on a long downhill slope. It gained momentum and for a second he could not pass, held in the slow spin of the huge front wheel, the hot grind of the diesel, and far down the shimmering road he could see another car coming. The truck's wheel drew him to the side like the hypnotic gesture of a swaying finger. So this is it, he said to himself, and his whole body went quiet; he imagined the impact, the hurtle and crash as though some metal hand had crushed them all. Then he was past, the other car neared and shot by.

Bailey's hand jerked and he almost dropped his snifter. He saw Brody staring at him.

"Sleepy?" his brother asked, and Bailey could tell by the tone of voice that he wanted to ask more.

"It's been a long day," he said lamely, and as if to break away from Brody's gaze he walked to the edge of the porch where Edward was standing. "Does it still work?"

Edward looked at him blankly.

"The telescope. May I?"

Edward held up his hand as if he had forgotten what he was holding. "Of course."

Bailey put his glass down on the top step and laid the cold rim to his eye. Suddenly a bright point of light wriggled into the black and seemed to split into three or four pieces as if exploding. The telescope had not changed, and he could no more make it work now than he ever could. He remembered his father's impatience when he tried to get him to see something. He could never hold it steady enough.

He felt a hand on his back and turned to see Jacqueline standing there.

"I think Lawson's fallen asleep," she said. "Don't you think we'd better wake him and go to bed?"

"Good night, everyone," Edward said from the doorway and they all murmured "Good night" to him as he turned and the screen door slapped behind him.

2

For a while Lawson had listened to what they said and watched Charlie Hutter, but when the conversation began again, not at all about Charlie or the wedding, he paid no attention. For a while he looked at his father who was not talking much, but most of all he tried to recall the face and figure of Bonnie. What came to him were not clear pictures of her at all, no matter how hard he tried to raise them, but bursts of her presence beside him at dinner or touching him under the tree. After a while even that did not seem clear, but he went over everything as often as he could. A bug made a plinking sound against the light bulb. In his mind the tree became a dark shell. He could hear himself breathing and tried to hold it in, listening for hers. He was under the lip of a diving bell and she swam dimly in the air beyond him. He began to run to her in slow motion, a wind pulling against him until he bumped his shoulder, which was the touch of his mother's hand shaking him awake and there was the porch again and Uncle Brody stretching and Aunt Esther leaned close, rumpling Lawson's hair.

"There, now, we've kept you up too late with our chatter."

His mother walked up with him and kissed him at the door to his bedroom. Edward was lying in his pajamas on the bed, hands folded on his chest, frowning at the ceiling. Lawson did not interrupt him but undressed and brushed his teeth. When he came back to the bedroom Edward was sitting on the edge of his bed.

"All set?" he said.

"Yessir."

"Good night, Lawson."

He barely had time to get into bed before the light went out, and he heard his uncle sigh and fold himself under the covers.

At first he was very aware of another person in the room, breathing and turning, and once his uncle sighed loudly and muttered a few garbled words. But soon the night outside with its small moon grew lighter, and the edges and corners of furniture humped into a silver glow. The bed was very soft, rising around his body in a plush way he was not used to, and the sheets smelled like the laundry room with its starch and detergents and the faint odor of a hot iron on linen. He was so tired that for a while he could not sleep, and his mind wandered restlessly.

Much later Lawson heard the sound of a car. He awoke so completely that he was not sure whether he had been asleep or not. Only the increased light from the moon showed that time had passed. He felt he had forgotten something important, and then, for just a moment, he could not remember where he was, or the shape of the room or where his bed was placed in it. When he heard the heavy, steady breathing of his uncle, the room gathered together. The crackle of the car on the driveway, the motor humming, made him sit up in bed, and carefully, so as not to wake Edward, he swung out of the covers, put his feet on the floor, held still for a moment, then stood as the old bed jiggled and squeaked. From the window he could see the car, its headlights slicing at his eyes, sweep under the window and disappear beneath the projecting roof of the porch, but in that brief moment he saw that one of the boys was driving, another girl was in the front, and Bonnie was leaning forward from the back to say something. Soft voices, a laugh. The car door slammed finally, gravel shot up against metal, and the car twisted down to the highway. Quiet came back. Then the tree frogs began to chirr again and suddenly a whippoorwill called, trailing on and on without pause until Lawson felt breathless. Whether she had come in or not, he could not tell. The house was silent and he heard no doors closing. As though a lid had fallen, the bird stopped and did not sing again.

Lawson started when he heard footsteps behind him. Edward put a hand on his shoulder and they both looked out into the night.

"Can't sleep?" Edward said.

"Nossir."

"I wasn't talking or snoring or anything, was I? They tell me I can be awfully noisy at night."

"I just woke up and came to the window."

Edward laughed quietly. Lawson leaned his head against the man's side. As always with Uncle Edward, he felt completely at ease.

"You're too young to start that," he said, and Lawson wondered what he meant by "that" and if Edward could see into his mind well enough to understand what he was thinking about. He was perfectly willing at that moment to credit his uncle with strange powers of vision, and it did not embarrass him to think that he might know.

They stood together for a while. The rim of the sky had begun to pale when Edward turned abruptly without a word and went back to his bed. Lawson wondered if he might have been dozing on his feet, so checked was the flow of his thoughts by his uncle's leaving. For a moment, with Edward's arm around him, he had heard in the chest he leaned his head against the muffled thud, and half-dreaming, he walked again with his father toward that model heart in the museum.

The heart was the newest exhibit. They had come to visit the Planetarium but it was closed for repairs. Bloated, red-veined, and shiny, it filled half of a vaulted room. When they were close, he could no longer see the whole of it, and the bulged, looming sides made it look like the inside of a whale's belly that he had once seen in a cartoon at the movies.

As soon as they entered, they could hear something beating, very heavily, like someone upstairs kicking monotonously, coming down with all his weight and trying to break through.

"This is the right atrium," and Lawson saw his father was reading a sign on the wall. "This is where the blood comes in from all over the body, Lawson. We're going to be just like corpuscles of blood."

Lawson did not like the sound and the dim light that was so red. The narrow tube they passed through looked as though it could pull tight around them like a snake. But on the other side, past a doorway made from two pink flaps of cloth that had to be pushed aside, they came to a much larger room. The beating was louder there.

"I don't like it here," Lawson said tentatively.

"Don't be silly. Here. There's a button."

Lawson let go of his father's hand and went to it as if floating dizzily in the red and shiny flesh. He pushed. From somewhere above them fell a very serious, low voice.

"This is the right ventricle. It is pumping. It pushes like an atomizer bulb and squeezes the blood up into the lungs. Behind you is the tricuspid valve. Above, you will come to the pulmonary valve. It is preventing backflow while the ventricle is filling."

By the time it was finished Lawson was wide-eyed and shaken. The voice sounded angry.

"Look, there," his father said. The wall was beating, beating.

He was pointing up the stairs at the far end of the chamber to the next flaplike door. "That's where the blood goes next."

The stairs were steep and narrow. The flaps, pendent as earlobes, trembled with the sound. Lawson did not want to hear. He pushed the button again, but was sorry when he had. "This is the right ventricle," the voice intoned, and he began tugging at his father, trying to run up the stairs.

"Here we are, Lawson." Bailey pushed on the door.

It was stuck. He pushed again. Only the red walls trembled slightly.

"Open it, open it," Lawson wailed.

His father pushed again, this time until he was flushed in the face. He grinned weakly. Lawson began to breathe in great sobs.

"I want to get out. This is scary."

"Now, now. It's simple. If the door's stuck, we'll just walk back the way we came and go out the front. Come on, we'll be backward corpuscles."

"No, no. I don't want to go back. I want to get out of this."

"Come on. I'll carry you."

"No."

He was screaming now. He did not want to go back to the pounding, the voice, like a dream of running and going nowhere.

"Easy, Lawson. Your daddy's here. You mustn't get so excited. Here. I'll just knock on the door. The guard will come."

He beat a few times on the door with his fist. The whole heart around them pulsed. In spite of its suffocating pulp, it seemed so fragile. Lawson began crying. He closed his eyes, held up his arms, and felt himself being lifted, the cheek against his, and rough patting of his father's hands. He was saying something quietly in his ear. Lawson clung as close as possible.

He did not remember how they got out, whether they went back or whether the guard finally came, and in his dreams again and again, or at times like this, standing by the window, it was as though he never had escaped, part of him still there, frozen in his father's awkward arms, the door closed to them both and the bloody, shining walls of the beating heart holding them swallowed.

Lawson turned from the window. He was very tired, so scoured out that he felt nothing. Somewhere a rooster was crowing when he pulled the covers over himself and by the time he had rolled once onto his side he was deeply asleep.

The moon shone so brightly into their room that for a while, when Bailey turned away from Jacqueline onto his back, he wondered if they had left a light on. She placed a hand on his chest, and still out of breath he lay staring at the sharply defined patterns of light and dark. He heard her say quietly, "I love you," knew she was already half-asleep, and pressed his palm flatly against her thigh. She shifted slightly to rest her head on her pillow and turned her face toward him for a moment, a heavy look in her eyes as though she had been drugged. She smiled, and the drowsiness of her face gave her expression a look so young that Bailey could see Lawson's face in hers, or her own as a girl, much younger than he had ever known her. He smiled back and she closed her eyes. All expression faded gradually, her hand jerked once against him, and then she was still.

She did not wake when he moved back to his own bed. For a while he kept glancing over at her. But in her sleep she was so completely separate from him, so unconscious of anything around her, that he began again to be aware of things that isolated them: the delicate bones of her skull, the thin layer over it of skin, the inconsequential tongue paralyzed in his own throat and never capable of translating the mind that moved it. He wanted to get behind the features of her sleeping face. If only he too could lie back now and sleep and leave his body behind as she had done, meeting her somewhere beyond the abandoned surface. They even made love by rote, bringing their familiar bodies to the same place again and again. Sometimes he felt as if their love were an endless falling, and they only held on in fear.

He had been so hard on her recently without meaning to be. But almost everything she did irritated him. She knew he was upset in some way, but her gestures of concern, a hand on his face, those eyes staring at him intently, only pressed against him, closed him in, and he would move away, snap at her, hide behind the closed door of his study. Only by taking two or three drinks before dinner could he get through the evening, the three of them eating their way through an increasingly tense silence. But that was dangerous because he had less control over his moods when he drank, and sometimes he would find an unlocated anger starting up in him, and he would rage almost incoherently, bitterly about some issue he knew really did not interest him: the ineptitude of plumbers, the idiocy of local politicians, the worthless dollar. After dinner he would go to the den, turn on the TV loudly so that no one could talk, and pretend to watch anything. But the drivel washed over him, his mind blank, until he was sleepy enough to go upstairs. Sometimes Jacqueline would come sit with him, and the sound of her knitting needles methodically clicking to one side would drive him up to his study again.

He had even struck her a few weeks before they packed up to go to the wedding. He had never done that before, and all his life Bailey had thought of himself as a gentle man, upset even by poisoning mice in their country house, not able to help his brother, Brody, in the slaughter of chickens or pigs. It was the evening after he had learned that he was fired. He did not tell her at first, but spent the afternoon in his study. At four o'clock he retrieved the bottle of bourbon. He knew he was getting very unsteady by the time Lawson slammed the front door, home from school. All the way through dinner he barely saw them, and he hated the way she kept passing him things, addressing questions to him that he ignored, pushing, pushing into his space. Besides, she probably knew anyway. He had told her weeks earlier that the city was having to lay off people because of the budget cuts, and that his office was going to be one of the worst hit because they certainly couldn't afford three engineers, but he had been shocked when Duffy told him, even embarrassed that he had never really expected it to be him. Lawson had hit a home run that day in baseball practice. Bailey tried to congratulate him, but somehow it came out all wrong, sounding as if he didn't think his son would do it in a real game.

When they left the table he started to walk back to his study, but she was close behind him.

"Bailey."

He stopped in the passageway, his back to her.

"Sweetheart, please, what's wrong?"

He wheeled, hands fisted at his sides. "They fired me. That's what's wrong."

He saw Lawson standing back in the kitchen, watching them from a distance.

"Oh, no. Bailey. How awful. They can't mean it."

"No?" He laughed bitterly. "They can and they do. Like that," and he snapped his fingers, increasingly angry at the melodramatic way he was expressing it, horrified that whatever emotions were forcing their way out now had nothing to do with the fact of losing his job, because although it had hurt his pride, he had realized that afternoon, well into the bourbon, that he would be relieved not to have to go there every day, and that what he had wanted for years could happen now—he could set up on his own as a consultant.

"Bailey. I'm so sorry," and she started to reach for him.

He backed off. "It doesn't matter anyway."

But she took that wrong.

"No. It doesn't. At least it could be worse. We don't have to worry about money."

He paled, the anger rising again, even though he knew she was trying to be reassuring.

"No. That never did matter, did it? Whether I worked or not. I mean, there's always that Ambler dough."

He saw the pain in her eyes, and that did it. Afterward he had to think that when his hand rose up and slashed across her face it must have been only to wipe away that look of pain, as if he could by the stroke of his open palm erase the hurt he had already given. She put both hands to her face, her eyes wide. Luckily the blow wasn't hard because he had managed to draw back slightly even as he swung. Past her face, in the kitchen Lawson stood gawkily, his arms risen from his sides as if trying to catch something about to fall. With a wail Jacqueline ran up the stairs. For a moment Lawson and Bailey stared as if they were both looking not at each other but the space between them where she had stood. Then Bailey's whole arm began to tremble. "Oh, my God," he muttered and ran up the stairs after her.

It was almost a week before she would have anything to do with him and no matter how fully he explained to Lawson that sometimes people became so angry that they lost control, the boy was very quiet and seemed even to keep a physical distance between them. But soon she forgave him. There were so many reasons for it, and he could tell she was so eager to have fixed causes for his behavior that he agreed with her analyses, invented others. She understood, but wouldn't he please get some help? Just see Dr. Figueras once or twice? He had been so helpful to her that year she'd had those miscarriages. Bailey found himself entering a new phase where he could feign calmness and well-being on the surface just to be left alone in his own anguish. Anything to be rid of their concern that pushed against him. Of course he would see the doctor. He went a few times. Both he and Dr. Figueras knew the futility of it on their first meeting. There was no way to help him if he did not want to be helped. The doctor was a good friend of the family so he had a few simpleminded suggestions for Bailey, a few even more simplistic terms to apply to Bailey's mental state, but Bailey thought even Dr. Figueras was relieved when the three meetings were over. "It's really nothing much," Bailey said halfheartedly, but for the first time Dr. Figueras looked firmly, even angrily at him and said, "But more than you can really handle, I suspect," and they parted on that, Bailey a little shaken since he had never thought anything was totally beyond his control. But then he decided that must be a gambit to bring him back to more sessions, to make him feel helpless. What he told Jacqueline was simply that the meetings had helped, he felt much better, and Dr. Figueras thought him capable of handling it now.

But he was confused and from that moment very circumspect, watching his gestures and moods carefully for anything inadvertent. That was when a sense of danger began to come over him. His dreams, vague, fluctuating, would hang ominously into the day, or he would wake suddenly at night, heart pounding, certain someone or thing was prowling in the empty house below, and for the first time he began to think of going away, of removing himself from the people he loved for a while because he might be dangerous to them. But then, what would he do without them? So one hand was held up and pushed Jacqueline away, and the other clutched at her possessively, and he dreamed of falling, tumbling like that forever. When the call came from Esther and Brody about Bonnie's wedding, he was surprised that he wanted to go back to the farm, wanted to have the bustle of his family around him—something he had always disliked before.

Jacqueline stirred once, whispered, but did not wake. He knew he would not sleep. He could hear the collar of a dog jingle as it shifted around on the porch below. The house always smelled the same, and half-closing his eyes he could remember what it was like to lie in his bed as a child, the house cupped around him. But for some reason he did not find that a comforting thought now, and he chafed at himself for being so sentimental.

After a while when Jacqueline's breathing was deep and steady, he rose quietly from the bed, slipped on his bathrobe, and walked in bare feet down the hallway to the stairs. He stood looking into the room below, dark except for one sharp wedge of moonlight that thrust itself against the side of a table. Then he walked down and stood at the porch door. One of the dogs rose to sniff at him from the other side of the screen, his tail wagging. Standing at that door in the dark reminded him of that hot and humid night in the summer when Jacqueline was carrying Lawson, dark except in the flashes of heat lightning that kept revealing the open and uncurtained window of their bedroom, and he had listened to his father walking the porch, back and forth, each booted footfall exploding in the heavy air. Sometimes the sound stopped, and waiting in the silence for the walking to begin again made him so tense that Bailey rose at last. "Where are you going?" she whispered tightly. But he could not answer. Even her question nettled him. Again the dark cracked for a second and he could see the slope of roof under the window, the mass of wide and motionless oak tree beyond the lawn.

Downstairs a lamp was burning in the parlor, revealing the squat and empty easy chair and section of worn carpet. He had stopped at the door to the porch, one hand spread on the screen, just as he did now. The figure of his father was walking by slowly, muttering. Bailey could make out none of the words. The footsteps halted, then began returning. The lightning flicked out, projecting his father on the mesh of screen naked to the waist, his thin hair awry in wisps, the bottle in his hands, and he was dressed in worn jodhpurs and riding boots. One hand was on the back of his neck as though forcing his face to turn down to the porch in anger. The image went slowly from Bailey's eyes back into the dark. He had wanted to thrust the door out and away, to grapple with that lean and surprisingly lithe old body. But he could not move forward or speak. His fingers made the screen sag as though a moth had fluttered against it. The footsteps had stopped. Bailey waited for them to come back.

But they did not. A short while later he heard hoofbeats approaching, jumbled and hollow, and in a flash of the lightning saw the old man leaning forward over the neck, still half-naked, the horse bunched to leap, and then the sound of hooves broke over the house and into the distance. He did not see his father again. He was not awake when they left the next morning. Two months later, a week after Lawson was born, the old man had a stroke. "It was too hot. He shouldn't have been riding in that meet, we told him," his mother said again and again in the evening after the funeral. "I told him it was just too hot." Three years later his mother died at the home of relatives in Atlanta. They let her be buried there. "She said she wanted that," Brody had said. "Mother told me she didn't have to be near him after she died." Bailey knew what she meant. After all, she had been at least that distant from her husband even when they were alive.

But that all seemed to belong to another whole lifetime. He put his hands in the pockets of his bathrobe and leaned against the doorjamb. Sometimes he dreamed that a man was gesturing at him from the other side of a deep moat, and then he would see it was himself, or once in a while, his father. Was it really his own father who had been the way he remembered him, surrounded always by those vague hints of scandal, of other women, gradually collapsing at home, alcoholic, quiet and even sly, yet often bursting uncontrollably onto the countryside at night, an old man who would wander from room to room by day, tall and gaunt, his slippers making heel slaps on the floor, sometimes standing in the doorway where Bailey or any of the family were, frowning as though listening to something on the other side of the conversation until all speaking died and they too listened for what he was hearing?

At the bottom of the field the headlights of a car flashed directly at him and then began winding up toward the house. Through the screen door he watched the car approach, saw it pull up near the porch, and listened to the voices. He could see Bonnie clearly, and the other girl who had been driving that afternoon, but it wasn't until Bonnie said, "Oh, Nora, stop teasing," that he remembered her name. But that was often true for him, especially with women. He never forgot a face, or the shape of a lovely body, but names eluded him. He watched them chattering to each other. Women, women. Ever since he could remember he had felt much closer to them than to the boys or men his own age. Probably sensing this, Jacqueline often kept a jealous eye on him, and he knew she suspected the worst. It was hard to reassure her, and he had become so aware of her watchfulness that self-consciously he would not look at a woman on the street if they were driving together. But he was irritated by the way she would follow him around at parties, and if she found him talking to another woman, she would stand there for a while smiling, then introduce herself, "I'm Bailey's wife, Jacqueline." Oh, there had been close calls, like that silky little blonde in Payroll who went out to lunch with him all the time, and he did go up to her apartment one evening, but they only kissed a few times and talked for hours over some wine about their problems, parting awkwardly late that night as if they both did not want to show what they had in mind. He had stopped seeing her immediately. It would get too complicated, and besides, listening to her talk that night, he had realized they had nothing in common. But he wondered sometimes if the other men around him were the same, or whether he was obsessed. Almost any woman he saw he thought of making love to. His friends talked a lot. He didn't, and even hated that locker room joviality. He just imagined.

The car spun away and Bonnie was standing on the steps waving at them. Bailey thought of saying something but he didn't. He was silenced by the way she stood for a while with her back to him and hand still raised, less as though she were waving than trying to hold onto something in the air. Then she sat down on the top step and leaned her head against the pillar. He heard the whippoorwill's crazed fragment and for a while he watched her sitting there, unmoving, and wondered what she could be thinking. Then he looked beyond her to the rolling, silvered field, down past the gateposts to the dark bank of trees, to the limits of the land where the stars began, looking at what he knew she was looking at, until he began for the first time that night to feel sleepy, and quietly, without saying anything to her, he turned and went back up the stairs to his bed where Jacqueline still breathed easily in and out like a reed in the passing wash of small waves.

3

"And this whole new row of stanchions I put in last October. But I guess I wrote you about them."

"Yes," but Bailey looked down the length of the barn not recalling any such thing. It could have been imbedded in one of Brody's rambling, gossipy letters. He always passed them on to Jacqueline and she would relate a condensed version to him.

"But there've not been too many changes for all that, have there?" Brody said as they strolled along the center aisle, cows lifting their heads as they passed, the metal ringing dully. "I've tried to keep it much the same. I think of it as not just ours, you know, but part of the family's. I mean all of us Wrights, and when the cousins come through, you'd be surprised how many of them take pleasure in seeing it as it was."

Bailey listened, doing his best to answer here and there, and Brody lapsed into a long account of how some second or third cousin had come by. He knew the family, all of it, down to dates of births and deaths, and loved to wander in the family tree, touching its limbs with a pleasure that Bailey could not understand. All that ancestor worship was suffocating to him. But he had long ago come to see it as a form of security for the elder brother, and even when they were very young, knowing the names and dates had given Brody his own place in the family, the keeper of the household gods.

"And you remember Aunt Sally May?"

"Yes," Bailey said, surprised that he actually did.

"She'll be coming to the wedding. Can you imagine that? How old do you think she is?"

They passed out the door onto the earthen ramp, and below them, standing with his hands clasped behind him and staring down at a chicken that was scratching at his feet, was Uncle Edward. He did not notice them.

"He's been all right?" Brody asked quietly.

"Oh, yes, just the usual. We know all the signs now, and Jacqueline or the aunts just drive him down to Tucker's for a stay when it starts."

Brody shook his head. "What a shame."

But Bailey did not like that almost patronizing tone coming from some sense of unshakable sanity. He wanted to say why? what's wrong with being loony and quietly slipping off to an asylum for a while; sometimes he wanted to do it himself, to be led like Edward gently into a waiting car and driven off to that large frame building behind its wrought-iron gate, where people were accustomed to his vagaries and he could be silent for days without anyone bothering him. But Bailey merely shrugged and began to walk down the ramp.

"Ah," and Edward looked up quickly. "There you are. Good morning, Brody. I'm afraid I was up very early and wandering a bit."

They chatted aimlessly for a while. The chicken strutted toward the others as if afraid they might have found what she was looking for. Bailey strolled off to the pigpen to watch the old sow rooting about in the mud. The sun was bright and warm, and for the first time that day he began to feel a lifting, as though the fresh breeze up and across the field, the new weeds already thick about the fence posts offered some hint of change. The piglets stumbled toward him as if expecting something.

He turned. "Edward," he called.

His brother-in-law paused in midsentence, hand lifted as if heavily emphasizing some point.

"How about a swim?"

"A swim?"

"Sure. I thought I'd walk on down to the lake. Join me?"

"All right. I'll get my suit."

"Oh, we can just jump in."

But Brody grinned and shook his head. "I'm afraid you'll find it's not quite as private as it used to be. You should see it on Sunday afternoons."

Again Bailey was annoyed. "Well, then, I'll get our suits," and he turned to the house, wondering how he was going to stay civil for long. But halfway back he had persuaded himself it was only the sleepless night making him edgy.

Brody walked to the fence and then waved them on. "I'm not much of a swimmer, Edward. Bailey was always the athlete."

For a while they walked down the red and runneled cart track in silence, Bailey carrying their suits and a towel. The sparrows chipped and flirted in the sweetbrier hedge and Edward looked intently at the pale blue sky as if reading something. Then he began softly humming some tune that never quite seemed to form itself, almost submerged in his breathing. Bailey watched a buzzard wheel off the ridge of Monument Hill, its gapped wings riding the currents.

"I was going to be married once, you know," Edward said as they left the fields and dipped into the woods that fringed the lake.

Bailey turned to him in surprise. He had so rarely heard Edward talk about his own past that he had almost begun to assume that he had little or no memory.

"Of course I was much younger. Twenty-eight at the time."

He paused.

"And you decided not to?" Bailey was afraid he would stop if not encouraged.

"Well, not exactly. She was only sixteen, you see, and my second cousin. The family did not think it right. My aunts were very much against it. That was before my problems began, but you see there had been some signs of it in my mother's family, and . . ." but he paused frowning. "Perhaps Jacqueline has spoken of it all, though."

"No, not at all."

Bailey could see the surface of the lake glinting now. Edward was smiling.

"But this is silly to remember. She was only a child and they were right. Her name was Betsey. She danced very well."

Bailey looked at the man's face. There was not the slightest hint of sadness in the voice or in his eyes, only a rather childlike joy, as if the mere memory of her dancing sufficed. Suddenly the man stood still and thrust out both his arms.

"When she danced, sometimes she danced like this," and stepping lightly on his toes over the hummocked earth, Edward closed his eyes, head slightly back and at a slant as if a long braid of hair hung down his back, and he began to circle with his arms outstretched. He teetered, started to fall, caught himself, and laughed, and Bailey could not help laughing too at the fleshy figure staggering into the pines on his toes, graceful in spite of it all. He stopped abruptly and Bailey caught up to him.

"She married a lawyer and moved to Birmingham," he said quietly and they resumed their walk toward the lake, this time in single file on the narrow path through the blackberries. Bailey thought it odd that although Jacqueline had often discussed

Edward's problems with him, she had never mentioned this Betsey who danced.

But the Amblers were that way, silent, almost conspiratorial about family legend, and when they spoke of someone the information was known to them but secretly coded. "You mean when Aunt Priscilla had her 'little moment' . . ." Jacqueline's father would say, and they would all smile knowingly; "which led to the 'problem,' " her mother would reply, and everyone would sigh. Bailey had admired this at first, coming as he did from a very different tradition where such an opening led inevitably to a long-winded recital of a story everyone had heard a thousand times before but loved to hear again, like children waiting for their favorite passage in a familiar book. He had come to hate that and to mistrust the way that Brody, even as a child, would pipe up with names at the right place, never telling the story himself, but never letting a detail get out of place. But after a while Bailey came to see that the Amblers' way was just another form of affectation—in their case an aristocratic belief that everyone in the community must be watching them, and it behooved them to keep the inner family disgraces secret, to be referred to aslant, delicately. He remembered finally being so annoyed that once when Jacqueline's parents came to dinner, early in their marriage but only five years before her parents both died, he of pneumonia, and she (languishing, they said) a year later, he had finished off the bottle of wine and interrupted their secret sharing to tell fully the most outrageous tale he could recall, the night that one of their workers, Hog Wilson, had been caught naked in the sheep pen and had said sturdily, "Mr. Wright, I don't have to waste no time courtin' 'em, and they ain't no back talk afterward." Jacqueline had almost gone home with her parents that night.

Edward paused in the woods to put on his suit, and Bailey walked out onto the beach. He did not see the figure of the girl lying there until he was almost stepping on her. She was stretched out on her stomach, the ties of her suit undone and back bare. She seemed asleep, not moving except for her breathing. Bailey cleared his throat, and she put her head up with a jerk.

"Oh," and she clutched at her halter as she began to sit up, her white breasts nearly bared. She tied the strings tightly behind her neck. "I'm afraid I was asleep." Then they recognized each other and said, "Why you're . . ." "Nora, isn't it?" Bailey said when she paused.

"Yes, and you're Mr. Wright."

Edward came out through the bushes in his suit and Bailey introduced him, then went back into the woods to change. When he returned she had combed her hair and was sitting on the neatly smoothed towel.

"I'm not used to seeing folks much here during the weekdays."

Bailey paused to talk with her. Edward had wandered into the water where he stood for a long time up to his knees, arms folded.

"Would you like a piece of my towel?" and she moved over to make room.

Bailey sat down. "Well, and how do you think your friend Bonnie is doing? Will she survive?"

"Oh, I hope so. She's very nervous. But I would be too."

"Why?" and he stared at the pert, blinking face, that nearly unmarred flesh of a young woman, trying to imagine which would begin to take over, the slightly pouting lines around the mouth or those more clever, furtive ones that curved about the corners of her eyes. He decided that if he was a young man, he would never trust her for a minute.

"Well, it's such a big thing, a wedding and all. All the people, and then the thing you're doing, marrying, and you know how Mr. and Mrs. Wright will just do it all up. Wouldn't you be scared? Or weren't you?"

Bailey paused. He had not thought of his own wedding for years. "I guess so. It's hard to remember."

"Hard?" and she put a hand to her neck. "Lord, I'm sure I'd never forget. But I'm never getting married, anyway."

"No? Why?"

"Married? Why get married? I've seen what happens to people after a while. My sister married and moved down to Jacksonville, and she has three kids and might as well be a slave or live with a washing machine. Who needs it."

Bailey grinned. "I don't imagine you do." But he was sorry he had said it because she blushed slightly, smiling back at him a little flirtatiously.

"Not yet," she said.

Edward broke the water with a heavy slap and they both turned to watch him splash out into the middle, his head pivoting slowly with each stroke.

"Well," and as Bailey stood he could not help looking down again at her upturned face and the cleft of her tightly bound breasts, "I guess if I'm going to do it before lunch, I'd better."

"It's been a pleasure talking. But I'm sure to see you again soon."

He smiled and walked to the water and without pausing dove in, shocked by the cold, then swam hard out toward the center. When he turned to swim back in she was already gone, and he was glad to have the beach to himself. Out in the middle of the lake Edward was floating on his back, kicking a little from time to time to stay up. Bailey dried himself and sat on the log that jutted into the water. Seeing Edward thrust and turn out in the center, he touched again on that guardian memory of the death, supposed to be as aimless as a misfired gun, of Uncle Eustace. This was one story no one cared to repeat, even Brody. Eustace was red-faced, swaggering, the life of the family, and salesman for a well-known soap firm. His company car bore its crest of moon and stars, and he always planned his route to bring him through the Corners for the big Fourth of July weekend when all the Wrights gathered at the lake for the picnic, fireworks, and drinking into late night when even children were allowed to wander and lose valuable hours of sleep. Uncle Eustace was noisy, unpredictable, the children's favorite because in his intemperate need to be seen in everything he did, he was most like them. The shorefront was his stage, the family his audience, and the children howled him on to grander and grander gestures. He could stand on his head in the middle of a picnic table, could set off firecrackers under the women's outhouse when Grandmother Wright was inside, could swim up behind a canoe full of young cousins and tip it dangerously to hear them squeal, would be reprimanded at least three times during the evening by Grandfather Wright, would fall for a moment into a state of almost weeping contriteness, but suddenly would be heard laughing again, perhaps breaking into some bawdy song near the group who had gathered by the fire to sing hymns.

But once when Bailey was hunting bullfrogs by the marshy side of the lake with a flashlight, he had come on Uncle Eustace standing in the water up to his shins, his arms folded, staring down at the black surface. Eustace winced at the light. "Hello, boy, frog gigging?" "Yessir." Bailey turned the light down, its dim circumference showing the way his uncle's flesh sagged over the belt of his bathing suit. He had a cigar in his mouth, but it was not lit. "You're Thomas's son, aren't you?" "Yessir." "Name?" "Bailey." "Bailey, of course." For a while they did not speak and Eustace seemed to have forgotten he was there. He sighed and lifted one leg briefly to scratch it, perched like a misshapen heron. Then he stood, quiet again, arms folded.

"Well, Bailey, do you like to sing?" "Yessir." "C'mere, then." Bailey went over to him. Eustace put a hand on his shoulder, very lightly. Bailey turned off the flashlight. The water was up to his thighs, cool, rising and falling slightly with the waves from some distant breeze. Bailey could smell the thick tobacco odor of the dead cigar and the sour mash of whiskey. "Let's you and me sing, Bailey. Softly, now. Do you know this song?" and quietly, in a very clear and thin tenor voice Uncle Eustace began to sing, "Go tell Aunt Rhodie." Bailey joined in, "Go tell Aunt Rho-o-die, go tell Aunt Rhodie that the old gray goose is dead. She died in the mill pond . . ." and they sang it to the end, then were silent. The hand did not move, a warm touch with hardly any weight behind it, voices came to them, some woman calling the name "Nancy, Nancy," and through the trees the campfire made a long rope of rippled light across the water. "Oh, well, Bailey, you'd best be about your gigging or the frogs will all be in bed." The hand lifted. Bailey stood for a moment, then went away. But he did not hunt frogs, feeling it was only polite to leave the cove to Uncle Eustace who, when Bailey turned from the point to look back, was still standing like a gray column off in the dark water.

Which was the way he preferred to remember him. He did not know how many years later he had died. It had been a hot day, humid with the threat of thunderstorms, but the heavy, dark clouds all passed to the south, and finally a cool breeze came, smelling of fresh rain. Uncle Eustace was without luster, unable to play his role although he tried from time to time, managing only to begin tricks and not carry them to their conclusion. No one scolded him. He talked bitterly about being a salesman to anyone who would listen. "Salesmen are bums," he said loudly. "Nonsense," Grandfather Wright said, but they were not really talking to each other at the time. He drank too much too soon and went to sit by the shore with a can of beer in his hand, a straw hat pushed back on his balding head and his scarlet face slightly dazed with heat and liquor. Bailey was going down to speak to him when Eustace rose, took off his shirt and with fastidious care folded it, put the can of beer on top of it, and placed his hat beside them both. He walked unsteadily into the water until it was over his waist and then began swimming toward the center of the lake.

Grandfather Wright said angrily, "He's too far out."

Eustace seemed to see them all watching. He waved with both his hands and his voice blew in to them.

"What is he up to?" and Cousin Martha came down to join them with a spatula in her hand. The children began to come too. Her little boy, Dan, pointed at Eustace and began jumping up and down. "There Uncle Eustace, there Uncle Eustace."

The voice was bellowing, almost angry. Grandfather Wright was shaking his head, the thin hand that extended from his starched cuff trembling with palsy as he clasped the arm of Harry, Martha's husband.

"Damn fool. What's he saying, Harry? Is he all right?"

They all became very still and heard, carried as clearly over the water as though funneled through a megaphone, "Damn you." Then again, "Damn-you-all-anyway," not with the offhand anger of a man nearby, but the clearly annunciated, sustained effort of someone shouting, each word separate and given a breath of its own.

"Lord," Martha said, and Harry laughed. The children who heard and understood were laughing too.

He began swimming away from them, then suddenly stopped and turned again, waved both of his hands as if to wipe away the lake, the beach, the sky, and then he disappeared.

Harry said, "Watch, just watch. He'll start popping up all around like a loon. Eustace can swim underwater in the durndest way. First one that sees him gets a nickel," and the children went to the water's edge to get a better view.

"He's hid somewhere," Harry said uncertainly after a minute. But they could all see that there was nowhere to hide.

Harry and Bailey's father, Thomas, and Uncle Porter were so tipsy that it took them a few minutes to get the boat down and into the water and after they had pushed off they found the oars were still back on shore and Martha had to wade out with her skirt clutched high. Then the women came down and herded the children away, but Bailey stood in the sand by the neat pile of shirt and hat and beer can, watching the boat sweep awkwardly out into the middle of the lake where it circled and rocked helplessly, and the men's voices came back to them on gusts of wind.

"He's only funning, Grampa," Martha said. "You know Eustace, he's just making fools out of the others."

But Grandfather Wright did not answer. His hands and head were trembling as he stared intensely at the boat and the men who began diving and swimming about.

The women took the children home and someone went into town to get the sheriff and a spotlight. They drove grandfather home at ten, and it was eleven before they found the body. Bailey was on the shore when his father came in, gaunt, still wearing his wet shirt and trousers. They did not say anything all the way home. Later that night, passing his parents' room, he heard his father say distinctly, "He couldn't have, I tell you. No Wright ever killed his own self."

Edward suddenly staggered up onto the beach, puffing and blowing. "Ah," and he stretched. "What a fine pond."

Bailey looked at him. Some kind of tension eased off. The man was so wet and happy, the sky behind his face was such a deep blue, and somewhere back in the woods a hawk was mewing.

"I'm glad you like it," and Bailey was proud that it really was his to offer, the water, the fields and trees and familiar mountains, all falling into place in his mind. A place to go, if only the illusion of a real past and its roots, if only for this one moment in the mind. It was home.

He could only smile. Sentimental fool, he said to himself, but as they walked back through the fields his heart was beating faster.

4

A truck had stopped under Lawson's window and he could hear Uncle Brody's voice. He could not make out words, but the laugh reminded him of all the other times they had come to stay. Lawson jumped out of bed, afraid that he had overslept. Edward's bed was empty. What if Bonnie had got up and gone off without him? He pulled at his clothes and then raced down the stairs, almost bumping into his aunt when he burst into the kitchen.

"Lord." She put her hand to her heart.

But Bonnie was not up yet. At first he stood on the porch where he could watch the bottom of the stairs inside at the end of the hall. But he was restless and began exploring the outside of the house. One or two holes were dug under the lattice of the porch and he decided to ask his uncle to let him lay out a coon trap, although possums might have made them. The spotted hound loped into the woods. Lawson took off his shoes and left them on the porch. Then he walked through the grass on the shady side of the house. The dew came up between his toes. He ran to the oak tree and dove into the high grass, rolling downhill under the branches where he stopped and threw out his arms and legs flat on the grass to stare up into the branches. He wanted to be up, high and away, and began climbing the tree, taking the next limb that he could reach and rising until the leaves were thin and he could see the sky clearly, and he was so out of breath that he could only cling there, the wind swaying him gently where he stood looking down at the lawn far below him, the upper windows of the house opposite, and then over the treetops to the river whitened by the sun. A single buzzard was high over him, dark and gap-feathered, and even though Lawson knew how ugly they were on the ground, scruff-headed and hopping, he envied its glide and slither. "Hi, you," he called to the bird, but it did not swerve or mark his voice in any way.

"Lawson. Here. In the window."

She was leaning far out of the second story, smiling, her hair tucked back by a blue ribbon.

"Hi," he yelled, and felt silly that he had shouted to the bird.

"You're up so high," she said.

He waved.

"Come down. I'm going to eat breakfast. Then we can go."

The branches shook when he moved. She ducked in and then reappeared, hands to her mouth.

"You still want to go?"

"Sure."

She waved and disappeared. He clung for a moment, a stiff breeze came and the whole treetop bent toward the house. For a second he thought his perch would snap and tumble, falling with a leafy rush. He climbed down fast to see how falling might feel and scraped one foot. But he did not mind. The grass was cool in the hot place where his skin had been burned.

He could hear her talking in the dining room, but he did not go in. From the tones of their voices he could tell that she and her mother were arguing again, so he waited on the porch and after a while she came.

"Emily's making us a lunch to take. Have you got your bathing suit?"

She was dressed in a blue-checked halter and tight shorts, her long legs bare and brown, feet sandaled.

"Yep."

When they climbed the fence beyond the lawn and dropped into the stubble of the first field a voice said, "Halloo," and they turned. Bailey and Brody were standing between the barn and the house. Brody was waving.

"We're going on a picnic," she called shrilly.

His father took a step toward them and then he waved too. At first they walked, but when the hill became steeper they ran down the old cart tracks. She began laughing and he was spooked to have her running just behind him so he laughed too and soon they were out of control, running loose-limbed. At the border of the woods he tripped and rolled and came up hard against a bank of tall grass, which did not hurt, and they both laughed even more. She pulled him up by the hand. Then they ran together. After a while she let go of his hand and slowed down. "I'm out of breath."

It was cool among the trees and the smell of night was still there. Soon she began asking him more questions, about his father and mother and Richmond but by the time they began to hear the river and the trees were thinning again, she was talking about herself and telling him funny stories about the people she knew, and he listened, afraid sometimes that he might not laugh in the right place.

They stood on the bank in the sun where the river was wide and shallow, turning on the rock bed with a windy sound.

"Come on," and touching his hand she began walking upstream.

Ahead the river curved to form a wide, smooth pool, and a yellow spit of sand spread gradually to the trees. By the woods was an old shack, leaning slightly, made of rotting logs. She dropped the bag and stepping out of her sandals, ran ahead of him and over the sand until she stood knee-deep in the clear, quiet water. She bent down, cupped and splashed the water over her face, and then shook her hands like a cat.

"There," and she waded back to him where he stood by the water's edge. "Isn't it perfect?"

She fetched the bag and handed him his suit. "You use the cabin. I'll put on mine here."

The door was around the back. He paused on the threshold for a moment until his eyes grew accustomed to the dark. The floor inside was earth, soft and damp to his bare feet. Two old whiskey bottles stood upright in one corner and the slant of the building made it seem to be falling. The beams and posts were thick, and the wall he touched was solid and did not give. One large crack in the roof made a bright slash of sun along the earth. He stood in it and took off his clothes, stepping quickly into his trunks.

He only wanted to be sure she was finished so that he would not come back too soon. When he looked through the window she was framed in it, standing by the water's edge, her back to him, and she was naked. He could not turn away. She looked up at the trees on the opposite bank, then putting her hands behind her head she stretched up on her toes, arching her back. She flung her arms out and he heard a small cry. Ashamed and afraid that she would see him, he stepped to the side of the window and leaned against the wall. He closed his eyes. When he opened them again and looked she had on her bathing suit, and then she ran into the water. He walked out, she waved and called his name, and he ran over the sand into the water that was so cold it made him ache. They swam together to the rock and she showed him the place to climb up. She sat with her knees clutched to her, letting the water run down her back from the wet hair, head back and eyes closed. Lawson lay beside her on his belly, his feet in the water.

She said something under her breath that he could not understand. The sun was strong on his back, the water a thin film of coolness. She leaned back on her hands and smiled at him.

"You don't talk much, do you? Mostly 'yes' and 'no.' I've never come here with anyone. Once I was going to show it to Charlie, but I changed my mind. It's always been my special place as long as I can remember."

He wondered if he should thank her. "I won't tell anyone, you know."

"I know. I could tell you're the kind who can keep secrets."

He pondered that for a moment and decided it was true.

"I'm not," she said. "It's funny, usually I tell everything. But that's one of the reasons I couldn't even tell Charlie about this. It's one of my last real secrets." She took away her hands and lay back on the rock, closing her eyes to the sun. "Do you have any secrets?"

Lawson thought he owed her one. He frowned, reaching out to put his hand in the water. "I don't really have any worth talking about. Nothing much happens like that."

"Nothing?"

"Well, nothing much. When I have secrets it's because I made them. Like just before I left home I buried a pen in the garden. It was a present from Aunt Fanny. But that's not really much of a secret because I'm the only one who cares."

He said that angrily because he had told her such an insignificant thing. She turned her face to him, shielding her eyes with one hand.

"That counts as a secret. Most secrets are yours more than anyone else's, anyway. I'll tell you something. I never showed Charlie this place because I was afraid he wouldn't really care. You see what I mean? I might bring him here as though it were something special and he wouldn't think much of it, so it wouldn't even seem special to me anymore. Does that make sense?"

He thought it did. Bonnie closed her eyes again.

"I'll tell you another secret, Lawson. Do you know what? I'm not sure I want to be married. Isn't that awful?"

Lawson was surprised. That did not fit in with what he had been told, how getting married was for people in love and people in love wanted to get married.

"Why?"

She sat up again. "You must never tell anyone I said that, will you? Because I will be married, and if Charlie ever knew . . ."

"No, I won't," and he was disappointed that she had to ask him.

"Oh, it isn't that I don't love Charlie. I do, I do. It's just hard to explain. I know he loves me, but sometimes I think it's like he doesn't love me at all. Because he thinks I'm someone I'm not. Sometimes he seems to think I'm so much better than I am and it's like he loves someone he wants me to be, not me. I don't suppose that makes sense to you. But you see, it means that when I marry him I've either got to be the way I am and disappoint him or else be the way he wants me to be."

She looked at Lawson and he was surprised to see how sad she was, almost crying.

"And I just couldn't stand that, Lawson. It would be like dying, like just dying."

She bit her lip. He did not know what to do. He was knotted up inside at the image of the man named Charlie Hutter whom he had seen only once.

"How come he's so mean?"

"It's not his fault. Don't you see? You can't be angry with him. It's my fault entirely. That's what is so awful about it. There's really no one to be angry at but myself."

He kicked his feet in the water. "I don't care. I saw him last night. I don't like him."

She reached out and touched him on the shoulder gently and then put her hand on the rock.

"No, Lawson, you'd like him if you knew him. Everyone does. He's quiet and gentle."

But Lawson vowed he would always hate him.

"Oh, I can't say it so you'll understand." Then she lay back again.

He held still, looked at her, and wanted to put his face against her but instead he rolled off into the water and swam around the rock, finally diving as deep as his lungs could stand it and then frantically kicking for the surface. When he climbed back onto the rock, she was sitting again and she doused her face with water. They both watched a flicker settle on a rotted tree and bob into an oblong hole there. When he turned back she was staring at his chest.

"What's that scar from?"

There was a tuck in his flesh below the heart as though a rib were missing.

"That's where I had that accident on my bike."

"Funny, isn't it? I'd completely forgot. And yet it was all Mother and Dad could talk about at the time."

"I forget too. It's all well now. But it's awfully ugly," and he put his hand partway over it.

"Nonsense. It's not at all. It's interesting, like a soldier's wound. Men aren't supposed to be beautiful like women. You know what? It makes you look older."

Lawson flushed slightly and looked away. He could not stop thinking of her naked and was certain that she would see where his eyes kept resting and would guess that he had spied on her.

"Let's eat," and she slipped into the water.

He tried to dive-bomb her but she ducked under. They tussled as they raced to the shore. It felt strange to touch her bare back.

They ate in the grass under the shade of a tree. After lunch they lapsed into a drowsy silence. Lawson felt no need to talk. Down on the beach again, she stretched out on a towel. The sun was hot. After a while he saw that she had gone to sleep, her face completely relaxed, her body still except for her breathing. He was nervous at first that she might open her eyes but when she had not for a while he stared at her. He did not understand the feeling in his body, the way he seemed to lean toward her, almost as though falling, his hands tense on his knees.

Suddenly he was afraid he might actually reach out and touch her. He stood up and walked the river's shore to the upper bend.

Around the corner he could see upstream to where the water joined at the stern of a small wedge of land. He clambered up along the rocks until he stood opposite it. Tall pines were growing on the island, leaving earth beneath clear and browned with needles. Lawson wanted to get across and tried to find a way over on the boulders but there was always an awkward gap too large for him to jump. Up to his knees in the current, he looked downstream but could not see the beach. She would not hear him if he yelled. Being alone in the tug of the river made everything feel slightly menacing, and he glanced once over his shoulder as though the noise of the river were concealing something.

Then he plunged in, swimming hard for the rock opposite him. But he had misjudged the current, which slanted him away and forced him to swim upstream. In the deepest part the water was dark; his feet groped down for a moment, touching nothing, and afraid that things he did not know were waiting for him, he flailed with his arms and could not get enough air. But then he struck hard against another rock, his feet could reach the bottom, and he was across. He lay down under the trees for a moment on the needles to catch his breath. Then he explored the length of the island, a quiet cool place heavy with the smell of resin. Instead of going back along the shore he decided to swim down the river to the beach. It was easy, moving swiftly with the current, pushing along in the shallow parts with his hands.

Bonnie was sitting up. He ran over to her, dripping water onto her legs.

"I went upstream. There's an island there."

"I know."

"I'd like to go camping there. I bet I could."

When she stood she had to put a hand on his shoulder and lean there for a second.

"You all right?"

"It's so hot it makes me dizzy."

"Come on into the water." He ran and dove in again.

She walked down until she was up to her knees and then she splashed her face. Suddenly she was taking off her bathing suit.

"That's better," and she laughed, tossing it high on the beach. When she turned he was staring at her but he looked away quickly. "Heavens, Lawson, haven't you ever seen a naked woman before?"

Lawson did not know whether he should turn away or not. She did it so naturally that he decided it must be all right and he did not want to seem inexperienced.

"Sure I have."

She plunged into the water and swam out to the stone. Then she called back, "Go on, silly. It feels great." He hesitated, then took off his suit under the water, tossed it at the shore, and swam over to the rock.

"Haven't you ever skinny-dipped before?"

"Sometimes," and he began laughing and took in a mouthful of water that made him choke.

She splashed him. He splashed back. Then they chased each other around the pool, finally to the shallow part where they kicked at each other.

"Oh," she said, "you're drowning me."

She tried to grab his head and push him under, but he wouldn't go. Instead she went under, and then they stood apart for a moment to catch their breath. He saw where she was looking and he blushed and turned away. She was laughing.

"Lawson Wright. You ought to be ashamed of yourself."

He tried to cover himself but she only laughed harder.

"Why?" he said angrily. He stalked over to his suit and began rinsing off the sand.

"Oh, c'mon. Don't be angry. I didn't mean it."

But he was furious now. He never wanted to see her again. Except that when he felt her hand on his shoulder and tried to shrug it off, he knew he only wanted to turn and look at her again.

"It just happens, you know," and he glared at the limp suit in his hand.

"I know. I didn't mean to laugh. C'mon. It's getting late."

She was walking away toward her clothes. His arms were tensed as though he had needed to hold onto her. As she stooped, her back to him, and began to dry her legs he hoped she would turn again and he did not care if she saw how stiff he was. But she didn't, and as she dressed piece by piece her clothes seemed to smother him.

No one was home when they returned. Emily told him they had gone into town and she gave him some lemonade. He went to his room. He did not want to do anything. How was he going to look and act the same to everyone? The afternoon seemed like days. But it was easier than he thought. The difference was mainly inside himself and he was surprised how they did not notice, even shocked to find out that he had overrated adults. He had thought they could see anything in him. His mother looked at him curiously from time to time, but she was only worried about how tired he looked.

At dinner Bonnie did not come down. "Poor thing, she's getting so nervous about it all," Aunt Esther said, "she's almost sick," and Brody shook his head. "Now, isn't that something? Who would have suspected Bonnie would feel that way?"

He went out on the lawn after dinner, waited for her to come out, and even kept looking at her window, but the shade was drawn and she never came down. Why was she hiding? There wasn't much time left. When his mother asked him to go to bed early, they had an argument; Lawson threatened to run off into the woods, and they both became upset. Finally Bailey had to take him firmly by the arm up the steps past his aunt and uncle and into his room.

He had calmed down by the time they came in to kiss him good night. He noticed how tired his father looked and that he smelled strongly like bourbon, but Lawson was in a hurry for them to leave him alone. Uncle Edward came in briefly to retrieve a book. As soon as the door closed Lawson went to the window and sat by it until dark came. Then he went to bed and tried to keep himself from sleeping, but he lost.

5

After a long day of gentle rain, the earth was left so soft that they had to put off raising the tent and making other preparations for the wedding, even though it was only three days away. All the petals of the fruit trees were washed down and the landscape turned shades of glistening green. Bailey wanted to be alone. He seemed to remember more and more things with clarity. Sometimes they were brought to mind by what he came across during the day—an old bit and bridle hung on a peg in the barn (for his father's horse, and even the jingle when he took it down seemed familiar), the smell of boxwood hedges pressed by sun (he remembered a day he hid from his nap after lunch under the hedge by the driveway on the crumbling, cool earth, hearing his mother's voice calling distantly until he fell asleep and woke to the flutter of two sparrows in the twigs above him), the rain on the roof of the barn as he worked in the loft high on the bales of hay. Sometimes images floated up out of nowhere, but always he was eager to take what came to him and he turned those fragments over in his mind until he wore them smooth, annoyed when people around him interrupted and dragged him back to the present.

To get away from them he walked alone up the shoulder of Sentinel Peak on the old trail that his father would ride, and only the best horsemen could make it up those last steep pitches to the top ridge. Toward the end of his life, only his father was good or foolhardy enough to want to. Now the path was washed into a streambed and saplings were choking the more level places. The leaves at the upper elevations were still newly uncurled, and Bailey paused from time to time to look down across the fields to the house and barn, beyond to the lake and the long, blue stretch of land east toward Richmond.

He took the trail down the other side, the darker slope where it was always damp. Growths of thick moss grew on the rocks and hung from some of the dead trees. As a boy he had often walked this trail up over the ridge and down the other side to the circling dirt road that would eventually take him home past the other farms, hoping to meet his father with his friends as they rode back. In places the old trail was hard to find. Now there was no trace of the bridge over the stream. The gutted path ran to the bank's edge on both sides. He poised on the bank, then leaped, barely reaching the other side, pulling himself forward by a sapling. Ahead he could see the red dirt road, too long neglected to be passable by a car, but where he sometimes had driven, and where he made love to his first girl friend, breathlessly pawing in the back seat of his car, which was followed by hushed, tense afternoons in someone's parlor, almost too eager to care if they were caught.

He stood there for a while, still able to smell that old car, its dusty upholstery, the surprise of how easy it all was and her small cries in his ear. If only it could stay that way—not the awkwardness, but the intensity, the obsessive wonder that made it impossible for him to think of anything but her body, her face lost in the haze of all those new senses. Even in the beginning with Jacqueline it had been that way. They couldn't keep their hands off each other. But at night now they moved together, perhaps for a moment connecting dimly to some former energy, but almost without pleasure. Maybe that wasn't fair. Maybe that was just himself. She always seemed ready, eager. But at times now her coaxing hand on his face or hip irritated him and he would rather have lain untouching beside her than be reminded of how dull it had become. Sometimes when he thought of Lawson, twelve, and with all ahead of him still, he was almost jealous.

Bailey walked on the crown of the road. When he had been young, four or five families lived along the road, mostly Issues, living in the two-storied cabins made of logs caulked with stucco, and always with a field to one side cleared enough to provide a small crop of corn, which filled a weathered, toppling corncrib, and to give some room for the pigs to root about. They were quiet, intense people. Or at least that was the way he always saw them because when he walked by they would stand still, expressionless, staring like deer who have looked up from grazing to study some unexpected sound. Dark-skinned and thin, delicately featured people, they made him feel like a trespasser who had violated posted land.

He wondered whose land this was now. It had rarely belonged to the Issues anyway. Passing around the next bend, he came to one of the shacks set in a clearing and still in better repair than the others he had passed. A split-rail fence sagged in front with a gate that hung open. He paused for a moment, almost expecting to see someone there. Only a flicker on the ground near a locust tree bobbed up from time to time out of the grass. But as he passed through the gate into the yard, he was uneasy as though the land itself gave off a sense of ownership. He caught himself looking over his shoulder. So the old sense of "mine and thine" was that ingrained in him.

For a moment, standing there, he could not see where the

door to the house was. No paths seamed the grass, and the house, brown-daubed and weathered, presented a blank front with only one small window in the second story. A tilted chimney of tin stuck up from the roof. He walked around to the side, startling the flicker that whirred off with a dash of white.

The door was on the other side, hanging half open. He looked back to the road, the torn gate and the woods growing thick to the roadbank. The house, unoccupied, was even more desolate because of the calm and half-overgrown setting. He pushed on the door. It was stuck. He tried to pull it closed, but it would not move that way either. Inside he could glimpse the rough floorboards and the corner of a soot-filled fireplace. The opening was wide enough if he turned sideways. He wedged himself through.

For a moment he held still, his hand on the door behind him. Every sound was amplified by the empty room. His own thuds and scratchings getting through the doorway had echoed as though someone else were making the same motions on the other side of the room. Now he could hear his own breathing, and when he moved his boots cracked old cinders and fallen pieces of plaster like a squirrel opening nuts. The windows were yellowed with dust and grime, some of the panes filled with cardboard in place of glass, and his eyes became accustomed to the light only gradually. A flame-eaten log pointed up in a mound of ashes in the fireplace and disturbed him the way it tilted, half-consumed. Bailey tried to imagine people living there but they were as transient as he was, coming into the empty, filthy place to perhaps spend a night or two and then pass on. He could not imagine the place clean, inhabited, warmed by the fire.

In the room off the back was a black-iron wood stove, one of its lids awry and leaving a dark hole. The stovepipe had come loose from the chimney and leaned back stiffly. An old table with one leg missing was placed against the wall so that the legless corner was thrust onto the windowsill, and the slim prints of coon paws speckled the dust beneath it. He did not like getting out of reach of the door, as if fearing someone could come silently over the lawn and find him snooping about. He was a man in an empty human shell, isolated, blank, remote.

A narrow set of stairs rose to the second story, so steep that they were scarcely more than a ladder. He climbed far enough up to heave his head and shoulders above the next floor. The ceiling was low and peaked, marred with tan cones of earth where mud daubers had built their nests. One window had fallen out, leaving only a hole in the wall. Something huddled in one corner of the room in a shapeless pile. Bailey looked down, past his feet to the room below, and then he went the rest of the way up.

He walked carefully into the middle of the floor, which cracked under him but did not sag. How could the whole family live in this one oblong room? But he knew how some of the people in town slept wrapped in their coats, on burlap bags filled with corn shucks. He went over to the corner. What he had seen were a pair of shoes and an old flannel shirt. The shoes were cracked and discolored with mud, the toes creased and turned up at an angle as though they had been kicked hard against stone. Ripped up the back and bearing a faded crisscross of stripes, the shirt was only a mutilated piece of cloth. Bailey could not take his eyes off them. Dumped there, hunched in the corner as though turned away from the empty room, they seemed the mute signs of some violence.

Across the window a dark object slashed once and by the time he had turned he only saw the view of the yard below, the light green leaves of bushes and trees. He held still, hearing the thrust of his own heart. Only a bird, he told himself, and caught himself saying the words over and over as though they were a charm. What was wrong with him? He was like a little child again. Peter Rabbit. Absurd. Yet he could not move, did not want to hear his brittle footsteps as though when he walked his own sounds covered the stealthy pursuit of someone else. He made himself walk over to the window and turned with his back to it to look at the room and the hole in the far corner, which was the stairwell. For just a moment he felt he had seen all this before, and that he was bleeding out into the dry plaster and boards, becoming flat, a mere decorative motif on a wall. When he walked to the stairs and down, the footsteps were like gunshots and he kept seeing flocks of small blackbirds rising startled from some gray field in his mind.

He squeezed through the door again, this time so hard that he dislodged it, and it flew back against the wall with a crack, small pieces of plaster cascading onto the floor. He did not close it but went out to the yard. There he paused to look back. Still nothing moved. The house seemed as unfamiliar to him as if he had not gone in.

Bailey sat down, his back against the fence. Strange how the unexpressed violence of the place took him back to one of his oldest nightmares. Or was it that harness he'd found in the barn? He knew the basic experience was real, but he had replayed it so often that he wasn't sure what was memory, what was imagined. He was sitting on the barn ramp, his knees tucked up to his chin. He must have been very young. He had been collecting the new, warm eggs from the chicken roosts in the barn. Half-dozing in the midsummer sun, the smell of his own sweaty legs and the manured dust strong, he heard the gathering jingle and stomp of the team of horses coming around the corner of the barn, and then his father drove into view, riding high on the harrow, the nervous horses bunching and pulling against the reins. His father was naked to the waist, burnished as he always became in the summer months, and as he passed, the bright blades behind him glinting, he waved. Suddenly the horses feeling the momentary lack of attention bolted, and Bailey stood, watching his father topple slowly from his perch onto the ground, the reins tangled to his wrists dragging him just out of reach of the blades, and the horses, panicked now, raced around the corner and out of sight.

Either they stopped or his father controlled them again. Bailey never knew. That happened out of sight, so for him the nightmare moment of descent was frozen forever, the lovely precision of danger held in check, rider in harmony over the animal and honed device, and the plummet to flailing hooves and a hundred sharp suns.

He shifted slightly against the old railing so that his face was in shade. That had become an image for the way he dreaded peaceful moments almost more than the painful ones. He did not trust harmony. It was only concealing something that could break out at any moment. He knew that made him overprotective with Lawson. How often he caught himself saying, "Be careful." His only son. He had found it almost impossible to be around him when he was an infant because he looked so fragile, and Jacqueline never understood why he would leave the room when the boy was beginning to learn how to go down stairs. He remembered that awful morning he had been left with Lawson. From his study he heard a wail and ran out to the garden to see the child had found a bottle and broken it on the stones and the jagged edge had cut deeply into his ankle. Lawson sat there, unable to talk yet, a continuous thin wail coming out as the blood smeared over his foot.

Well, after a while Bailey had learned to deal with that. Lawson was a boy, and there were constant cuts and bruises. Finally he saw that harder things had to be worried about. Earlier that year he had leafed through a college alumni magazine, and there was a picture of Al Close, a roommate for one year, and he was a bank vice-president now, but how old he looked—half-bald, a set of lines that Bailey would not have guessed the face was to receive. But Al was his age. Later that day he saw himself in the mirror and stopped to look hard. It had to be true of him too, only he couldn't see it. But after all this time, what did he have? What had he done? What could he say he was passing on to Lawson? Some money from the Amblers, a house in the city bought by his small Wright inheritance. He had done nothing to show. Even when Lawson fell into times when he needed to understand something, and that would come soon, what could Bailey do to help him? He sometimes felt he knew nothing, had no understanding of anything in his life. He was starting all over again, but he was tired, very tired.

Bailey stood up. He muttered, pressed his hands to his eyes. Jesus, what nonsense was this, flagellating himself in some empty field. But even as he said it his mood swung back and the words tolled like the clapper in a cracked bell—only child, only wife, only husband, only life, only, only—and he shook his head like a dog leaving water. "Quit it, quit it," he said outloud.

He walked on down the old road, trying to connect again with the warm late afternoon, to rid himself of the sense that he had done something wrong, and he took long strides, working up a sweat. He could never walk out of any place without feeling he had left something behind, and he always paused on the doorstep in the morning on his way to work, touching his pockets to make sure everything was there. Jacqueline teased him for being so cautious. By the time he had come to the gravel road leading to the back end of the property, he was thinking only of what he would do that evening. When he glimpsed the barn he broke into a trot to see if he could run that far. He sprinted the last hundred yards, surprised at how easily the ground unrolled beneath him, and stopped in the doorway to the barn to lean there, very winded but sure that he could have kept on going.

He had let himself get in such poor condition gradually. He breathed deeply and stepped into the long aisle of the barn. That was what age was—you let yourself grow old. But it wasn't too late. He reached high to a beam over an empty stall, grasped it with both his hands, and chinned himself once. His arms did not even tremble, his back strong and tight. He walked through the barn to the other doorway and the ramp down to the yard, breathing the smells of manured hay, the sweet rot of milk where it had spilled over, all the rich abundance of animals. The stalls were empty now except for one horse that shifted nervously as Bailey passed. In the last stall he paused to urinate, arching freely onto the back boards, and he laughed remembering how he and Steven Sargent used to match streams on a hot summer afternoon.

When he came around the front, he saw a car there, a convertible, the engine running although no one was in it, and recognized it as Nora Smith's. Then he heard voices and Nora and her brother, Billy, came out onto the porch, talking to someone inside. Billy turned and went down to the car but Nora was still talking. She stood with one hand shading her eyes as though the interior of the house were very distant. Bailey stared at her. She posed as though facing a photographer. But then she turned, saw him, and said, " 'Lo, Mr. Wright," and walked around the car to where he was standing. Lawson came out from behind the screen like a shadow. "I was hoping to see you."

She was being too birdlike, her chest thrust forward, eyes blinking rapidly. Her brother stared back up to where Lawson leaned against the porch pillar.

"What can I do for you?"

"Well, I'm taking this course now. It's in math. I had to make it up, and I'm having a time. I mean it's something awful, and your wife said maybe you'd give me a little tutoring. I didn't know you were an engineer till Mrs. Wright told me."

She paused for breath.

"I mean, I'm awfully dumb, and I wouldn't ask you to help me like this because I wouldn't even ask my best friend, but I've got to pass this course, I've just got to." She reached up suddenly to pull at the strap of her halter, which had begun to slip. "I'm hoping to go to nursing school next year."

As she was speaking something worked its way slowly through Bailey's mind. He glanced once at Lawson. He and Billy seemed to stare at each other, Billy's jaw working over the gum in his mouth. He could not help comparing Nora to Bonnie, and he was surprised how unflattering that was to Nora. She was not any less attractive. What was it then? She was standing there, waiting for him to say something. *Dumb* was the word. She had used it herself. That was it. He had never realized how bright Bonnie was until now. Always with Bonnie he had the feeling that at her most opaque moments she was merely acting dumb, that she took on the characteristics of one of those pert belles just to give herself time to think and feel inside without showing anything. But this girl Nora was that type in the flesh. He looked at her frankly and put a hand on her arm.

"I'd be glad to."

"Oh, would you?" She smiled back, he let go, and as she stooped into the car past the door he opened for her, he smelled the lilac and jasmine of her perfume. "I'm going to hold you to that, Mr. Wright."

"Please do," and he leaned slightly into the car after he had shut the door with both hands. He could not help looking at her legs and if she noticed she did not seem to mind.

"Say good-bye to Lawson, Billy," and she turned suddenly toward the back seat. But her brother did not say anything. "Bye, Lawson," Nora said. Suddenly Bonnie was at the window above and the two girls hooted at each other.

Lawson stood away from the pillar, both hands in his pockets. "Bye," and he looked at her so hard that it was obvious he did not want anyone to think he had weakened enough to say good-bye to Billy.

She called, "I'll bring my books." Bailey said, "Do that," and the car moved off down the driveway. He went up to the steps. All around the front lawn were piles of chairs and tarpaulins and poles.

"Well, did you have a good time?" and Bailey put his hand lightly on Lawson's shoulder as they went back into the house.

"No."

"Why's that?"

"Because. He's a jerk, that's why."

Bailey leaned back slightly and laughed. He didn't know why.

But Lawson started laughing too and when James ducked out of the kitchen to see what was going on he seemed to catch it from Bailey, and before long all three of them stood laughing uncontrollably in the long shadows of the late afternoon.

6

Still half sleeping, Lawson heard strange poundings and men yelling and then the rush of a motor rising and falling abruptly. He sat up and rubbed his eyes, then clambered out of bed to go to the window. The lawn and field seemed turned and twisted since the day before. A large section of fence had been yanked out and its stakes and poles lay piled to one side. A van had backed partway through the opening and the driver was leaning far out of his window to see behind. Mired in a small ditch between the driveway and the field, the truck roared and spun, rocked forward slightly, and then back, spewing clods of earth. A smaller truck was parked under his window and Negro workers in soiled white jackets were pulling out ropes and stakes and slabs of tabletops. Some carpenters in pocketed smocks were pounding together a heap of fresh, yellow boards. Next to the fence a green and white rectangle of tarpaulin was dumped with tangled coils of ropes piled on it as though to hold it down, but it billowed at the corners in the breeze like a nervous kite. Uncle Brody stood on a pile of folded wooden chairs, face puffed red, and he was waggling his arms at the truck like an angry conductor. As if brooding over the confusion, his father stood against the fence with arms folded. Both were dressed in work clothes and for a second Lawson had not recognized Bailey. Leaning far out over the sill he stared with his mouth open, and then it all came back to him: why they were making such a mess, where he was, and above all the fact that the wedding was only a day off. He had to find her.

He tumbled back into the middle of the room, already half-naked and looking for his clothes. Edward was gone, his bed smoothed as though he had never been there, and Lawson felt betrayed. Why didn't anyone wake him sooner? Even if the look of the sun told him that it was still early in the morning, he had lost precious hours. How in all this hubbub would he find a time or place to be alone with her? He did not know what he would do, what he wanted to say, but he had to be alone with her again. Already two days had passed, and she had been so shunted about and occupied by the women that he hardly ever saw her, and besides Billy had hung around all yesterday getting in the way. He paused with his pants half on. The engine suddenly cut off and the voices, still yelling, were frail without the motor's chug beneath them. What he heard now for the first time was all the shifting and pounding inside the house, voices on the landing, footsteps passing, women yelling from one floor to another. His own room was a silent box buffeted by currents of noise. He finished dressing, clung for a moment to the doorknob, and then went out into the hall.

At once he was brushed by a man passing with two long, white boxes.

"Heads up," and the man careened down the hallway.

An elderly lady was standing over two Negro girls who were sitting on the stairs winding long-stemmed flowers between the banister palings.

"The wax vines," she said testily. Neither girl looked at her. "Hurry, now."

Lawson tried to squeeze past her but she put a hand on his arm without looking at him.

"Diane, Diane, careful, you're going to break that stem," and as though it had been an order the girl snapped it in her fingers and looked up, her cheeks sucked in and eyes half-closed. "There, I told you, oh, you girls, will you never learn? Here," and she shook Lawson's arm angrily. "Bring up those boxes of vines, boy."

"What boxes?" Lawson said.

He peered down the stairs to the hall below. The railing was half-decked as though a vine had wound upstairs in the night.

"Hello," and the woman removed her hand. "You're not the florist's boy at all."

"No, ma'm."

"I am so sorry." She put a hand to her head. "Mercy, things are just so confused. Doris, go on, child, get those boxes," and she spoke so severely to the girl that Lawson wondered why they weren't both in tears.

He passed them and went down to the hall where heaps of cartons and various chairs had gathered since he went to bed. While he was standing on the bottom step, James wedged through the front door, four very oblong boxes stacked in his arms so he could not see Lawson. He groped with his feet at each step and was muttering something over and over under his breath.

"Hello," Lawson said when he was beside him.

The boxes shifted but held.

"Oh-oh," and then James smiled and nodded, but he kept going, laughing quietly to himself, and disappeared through the swinging doors to the kitchen. For a second Lawson saw figures moving about, the face of Emily with her hands to her mouth and her voice was saying, "Law', James, what you doing?" and the door swung to, cracked open briefly again to show the whole pile slanting away from James, and then a series of thumps were muffled by the closed door. Someone else whirled in the front, running lightly.

Nora stopped by Lawson and smiled.

"I'm late, is she angry?"

"Who?"

"Bonnie. Isn't she up yet?"

"I don't know."

She spun around to look at the boxes and chairs and then came up onto his stair.

"I wish I could stop and chat, but I know she's going to kill me. I promised to be here an hour ago to try on my dress. Is your aunt upstairs?"

"I don't know."

"Goodness," and she giggled as she began going up, "you just don't know anything, do you?"

She was already at the top of the stairs. "Mornin', Miz Wailes," she said as she passed the old lady on the landing above, and the woman replied, "Why, hello, Nora, how's your aunt?" and Nora said, "Jes fine," only by then her voice was very distant.

Lawson skirted a pile of boxes and edged into the dining room. There everything seemed composed and calm. The doors to the back veranda and garden where no one was working were open. Place settings of newly polished silver and glassware that reflected the checkered light were on the table. But he did not want any breakfast and left to pause again and listen at the bottom of the stairs. So many voices, doors opening and slamming, footsteps making the floors creak above, yet he could not make out what he wanted to hear—her voice, some sign of her presence, even if only someone calling her name. The flower lady was still scolding (they had moved on to the first floor now), some men soothed their way through heavy moving ("Here, here now, to me," "Easy there, steady," they chanted), his aunt was calling a name (it sounded like "eagle, eagle," but he knew it wasn't), Nora was laughing as if she could not stop, and then a door slammed as though the wind were trying to tear it off its hinges. He stood there, his fists clenched, leaning forward slightly, and he might have been about to attack someone who had insulted him.

He felt insulted. She was too busy, too happy to think of him. He was suffering, suffering. It was her wedding, her party, and no one cared what happened to him. He could go off and drown in the lake and they would never miss him. Not until dinnertime maybe, when they would discover his empty place—everyone waiting, a silence coming over them all, Bonnie whispering happily to Edward, then someone would come, a farmer maybe, "We found him washed up on the beach," description of his death, wails and groans, his parents in tears, then the body, pale, clothes torn, borne in on a flowered litter.

The bell rang once. Then it rang again for a long time. James swung out of the kitchen, buttoning his white coat. He opened the door for a stout lady, wearing a doughnut-shaped hat, and with her she had a Negro woman carrying a box.

"Mercy, I thought no one was home." She spoke as if to a large group of people just beyond James's shoulder.

"Yes'm."

"Mabel, Mabel, is that you?" Aunt Esther was at the top of the stairs. Jacqueline was looking over the railing.

"Hallooo," and as she entered she shed a pair of white gloves.

Aunt Esther came down quickly and Lawson's mother followed.

Esther said, "Have you got it?" and the two women grappled with each other on the bottom stair.

"Jacqueline? Is that you?" and they took a turn at squeezing too.

"It's Mabel Chipley," Esther called back up the stairs to Nora who stood at the top dressed in a slip, her hair down around her shoulders. "She's got the dress." She started to urge the woman up the stairs by the elbow.

"I do hope it fits," she was saying to Jacqueline, but that was when his mother caught sight of Lawson.

"Lawson, is that you?"

He was standing among all the boxes. The woman looked over her shoulder and Esther peered at him.

"Why, so it is," she said. "Come here, Lawson, and meet Miss Mabel Chipley. You remember Lawson, don't you?"

Lawson shuffled to the stairs. The woman, two steps above, extended a pale flipper to him, stiff as a dolphin's. He shook it.

"Where is your father?" Jacqueline said.

"Outside."

"Well, you go on out too. I don't want you in the house getting under foot. Have you had your breakfast?"

"Yep."

"And you're not to use the toilets much because they're backing up and the septic tank is plugged."

"OK, OK."

He saw his mother hesitate as though she wanted to come down, but the other two had turned, she was in the way and had to go first, so she looked once at him then turned to accept Miss Chipley's hand on her waist and went ahead of them, a piece of driftwood being pushed by a two-headed wave.

The wounded engine squealed and backfired into silence. Lawson ran down across the lawn, past the partially set-up table, to the mired truck. The driver was draped into the open hood, the upper part of his body already devoured by the beast. Uncle Brody stood on the front fender leaning far in with his hands in his back pockets.

"Uncle Brody?"

"Hi?"

He looked around but did not see Lawson so close below him.

"Uncle Brody."

"There you are. What is it, sonny? Can't you see I'm busy?"

He had not shaved and his face was streaming with sweat. He said a few other words quietly that Lawson could not catch.

Lawson strolled back across the lawn as far as where the men were putting up the tables and then stopped. He could see his father helping to pound in the tent pegs. The tent was up now, a long pinnacled piece of mottled canvas. Esther's friends from the Garden Club were already going in and out with flowers and cartons. A man drove his truck onto the front lawn and walked back toward Lawson with a shovel, pick, and ladder. He threw them down a few yards away.

"You ever seen a septic tank, son?"

"Nossir."

"Well, stick around and you will. You're just about standing on her."

Lawson moved and the man began digging. He heard the front screen door slam. There was Nora. She came out to the steps and looked around as though trying to find someone. Maybe she had a message from Bonnie. He tried to step clearly into view.

"Here, hand me that pickax, boy."

The man wagged a hand impatiently at him. By the time he had handed it to him, Nora had turned and gone. He wanted to run back to the house. What if she had not seen him? They would think he had gone away for the rest of the morning. He looked at Bonnie's window, but the shade was still drawn.

When the tent fell because a cow had got meshed in the main rope, it did not make any noise but sagged into a lump like an airless balloon. One of the women was standing where the entrance had been. She was yelling hysterically.

"Lyvia, Lyvia, my God, she's in there."

"Come on," the man said, and he and Lawson ran down the lawn.

The men began struggling with the canvas and had it rolled back in no time. Lyvia was lying on her back with her thin arms spread out as though she were sunbathing, but she was very pale and had her eyes closed. The other woman kneeled to take her head in her lap. Lyvia opened her eyes, breathed deeply, and then began moaning in high gasps. The men stood around with their hands in their pockets.

"Close call," Brody said.

"Can't you get a doctor?" the woman blurted. "Don't just stand there."

"She's all right. Just fright," and the other men agreed.

Lyvia opened her eyes. "I was like to suffocate," she said in a high, frail voice.

Brody shook his head and kneeled by her side.

"I am so sorry," he began but she burst into tears.

"I'm Lyvia Jester," she sobbed.

"I know, I know, I recognized you."

"I just came to help," she wailed.

"Well, wasn't that good of you," Brody said and the other woman rocked her gently in her lap. "Here, let's get her up to the porch in the shade," and two of the men took her by the arm on each side and helped her walk slowly over the lawn to the porch. The cow, who had looked on dumbly, lowed and began to struggle with the ropes.

Brody said, "Damn women," under his breath as he passed Lawson.

The rest of the morning was spent getting the tent up again and starting the truck. The man dug far enough down to disappear in his hole and still he had not found the tank. "I know she's hereabouts," he called up to Lawson when he passed the ladder down to him. Lyvia Jester was taken home because her nose had begun bleeding. The men drove off to eat, abandoning tools and lumber and tables, leaving a sudden quiet. Lawson passed the man in the hole his lunch. "It's cooler down here," and his voice was hollow and slightly muffled. Lawson waited eagerly for lunch. She would be there. His father and Brody climbed a pile of chairs and argued distantly about something. When the call came, Lawson waited for his father to catch up to him and then they went together. His hand on Lawson's shoulder was an absentminded touch.

Esther and Jacqueline and Mabel Chipley were already at the table and the soup had been poured into bowls. But neither Nora nor Bonnie was there and by the time the soup had been eaten they still had not come. Lawson was impatient and annoyed by the constant chatter and laughter. They all were so worked up and few of the things they said seemed worth laughing about. Finally he could not bear it anymore.

"Where's Bonnie?" he blurted, and his voice was so loud they all turned to him.

"Goodness," and Esther put a hand to her throat, laughing nervously, "what a shock. Was that you, Lawson? Why it sounded just like the voice of a stranger."

"Voice changing, eh?" Brody winked. "Growing up."

"Do you feel all right?" and his mother reached across the table and touched his forehead with the flat of her hand, but he drew back. "You've hardly eaten at all."

"I'm all right."

As if reading his mind, Brody said slyly, "I bet he misses his cousin."

Suddenly Lawson thought they all knew and were playing some kind of mean game.

"Now, don't be a tease," Esther said. "After all she is the only one who's paid any attention to him since he came. We haven't done right by you, Lawson. I'm ashamed. After the wedding, though, I'm going to see to it that things aren't so dull for you. Maybe we could see if Buddy Hawkins could come over to play."

"I don't want to play with anyone."

"My, my." Mabel Chipley peered at him indignantly.

His mother said, "Lawson Wright, you apologize to your aunt this minute."

"It's all right," but Esther's tone of voice indicated the opposite and she was buttering a piece of bread very hard. "I was pestering him."

"Lawson, you hear?"

Lawson did not care. He hoped they would send him away from the table, or give him an opportunity to say worse things. He would stick his tongue out at them all. He glared at Mabel Chipley who was staring at him over her glasses until her eyes grew big with shock.

"Mercy," she said under her breath.

A Negro man in black service clothes was standing in the doorway with a visored cap in his hand.

" 'Scuse me, but I was told to tell you folks that Miz Wright is here." His voice was without expression and he looked at no one in particular.

"Marshall? Is that you?"

"Yes, ma'm," and he glanced at Esther.

"Aunt Sally May is here?" Esther said. "Good heavens, I didn't expect her till tomorrow."

"Why not?" A voice came from behind the chauffeur, and when he stepped aside she wheeled herself up to the threshold. "Aren't I welcome?"

Esther shrieked, "Aunt Sally May," and the men stood, and one by one everyone took a turn at stooping and pecking the old lady's cheek. When she moved, a heavy necklace of purple beads rasped and clattered and she said nothing when they came one by one at Esther's calling.

"And this is Lawson, hasn't he grown?" Esther said finally, and Lawson went up to her, but as he stooped she put a hand on his shoulder and held him there for a moment.

"I should hope so. Haven't seen him since he was one." She had dark brown eyes and a skin much more wrinkled than Lawson had thought from a distance. Her lips trembled slightly all the time. "Fine," she said at last. "You may kiss me," and after he had, she let go of his shoulder and as though speaking only to him said, "He looks like Tommy."

"Doesn't he though?" Esther nodded. "I was just telling Jacqueline so."

"Where's the bride?"

"She's upstairs, Sally May," and Esther looked as though pride were going to make her cry. "You won't believe how beautiful she is."

But the old woman only nodded once. "You've gotten fatter, Brody."

"Stouter, I'd prefer."

She shook her head and looked at Bailey. "Fat. And you look older than you should, Bailey. You're still a young man."

Lawson decided right away that he liked her and the way she said outloud what she was thinking.

"Was it a hard trip from Arlington?" and Esther tried to get her attention.

But she would not let them off easily. She took them up one by one, even Mabel Chipley, and said things he could see they did not know how to accept. Finally she seemed through, and Marshall wheeled her as she commanded out onto the porch. "You come with me," and Lawson followed by the arm of the wheelchair where her hand was poised like a delicate spider.

But his mother came out and took him aside. She scolded him and told him he had to have a rest and made him go up to Aunt Esther to say he was sorry, and when he did, Lawson found it very hard not to get teary, but he managed to say it and turn away. He could see Aunt Esther looked touched. But Great Aunt Sally May (his grandfather's sister, it was explained to him) would not let him be sent upstairs, so he was allowed to rest on the porch divan while she sat nearby in the shadow of the lilac bush.

For a while everyone stood around and talked with her. But then she told them abruptly to leave her alone. "I want to rest too."

"But wouldn't you like to come to one of the beds in the back room?" Esther said.

"No. I always rested here. I like looking down the field, only I wish you hadn't cluttered it up so. I'll be off to Cousin Lila's later. Now leave me some peace and go about your business."

The women went upstairs again. Brody and Bailey were about to go down to the tent when the man came out of the hole in the lawn, pulled up his ladder, and sauntered to the porch.

"I'll have to be off now."

Aunt Sally May seemed to pay no attention to them. She was staring away to the oak tree and the woods, her face made ancient by its complete lack of expression. It reminded Lawson of a turtle, and he wondered if she could have gone to sleep with her eyes open.

"Off? Where to?" Brody looked at the hole and then at the man.

"Hose-and-Ladder. Got a meeting this afternoon."

"You can't leave that damn hole in the center of our lawn."

The man shifted his plug. "I'll be back this evenin'. I'll fill her up. I found that septic tank. Nothin' too wrong with her, except she was sunk too deep."

"This evening? I'll bet. I know those Hose-and-Ladder meetings."

The man smiled, then covered his grin with the back of his hand, ambled down to his truck to start the engine into a whine.

The men went back to work. The truck was freed and after a while it rumbled away down the driveway. Sally May was awake, but she and Lawson did not talk to each other, and from time to time she nodded and murmured to herself. From where he lay Lawson could see the profile of her aged face, and he stared at her. She was so unconscious of him that it did not seem impolite. The more drowsy he became, caught in the gentle shuttling to and fro of the divan, the more her face became the center of a darker area surrounding her and soon even that dimmed. Almost sleeping, he had fallen back into himself and was looking out very distantly through opaque windows. He felt feverish and languid and when people passed over the porch, going in and out of the house, he heard them through layers of silence and saw them only as shadows. None of them were as real as Bonnie and she shifted around in all the forms in which he had seen her, clothed and naked, smiling and sullen, and yet he could not touch her and she could not hear him. Later, through the screen of lilacs, he could see some horses moving toward the barn. The old woman leaned forward on the arms of her wheelchair, her chin thrust out. The full sun of the afternoon seemed to press bees out of the ground. They hummed and stirred in the lilac leaves.

He came back to himself with a jerk. Marshall was wheeling the old woman to the more shaded end of the porch, the sun was all aslant and he knew he would have to find Bonnie himself. For a second when he sat up he was dizzy. The divan was weaving in and out of the dappled light. Just inside the door he could hear his mother talking.

"So, you're awake," the voice of Sally May said, but he did not answer.

He met his mother in the hall. She was on her way back upstairs and turned when he called.

"Lawson. Did you have a nice rest?" She put a hand on his shoulder. "Now look, dear, while I have you alone for a minute . . ."

"Mother, listen," and the words pushed at him, not to confess, but to somehow make her his accomplice.

"No, Lawson, now you listen to me. We're all a little tired and confused and you've got to . . ."

"Please let me come . . ."

A man was yelling "Hey, hey," distantly, and someone was laughing in shrill, uncontrolled bursts.

"What . . ." Jacqueline said and then, "My Lord, it's Aunt Sally May."

They both ran out to the porch. A horse had strayed. He was in front of Sally May, not more than an arm's length away where she sat by the end of the porch. He was looking at her guiltily as he browsed among the banks of flowers there. She laughed with her hands clutched tightly to the wheels and her glasses hung by one ear across her face. Two men were running up yelling, "Gee" and "Haw" and everyone else seemed to have stopped to watch. When they got there most of the plants had been uprooted and the nasturtiums were mashed into the shape of hoofprints. One of the men tried to apologize but Sally May could not stop laughing. She was still laughing when Marshall wheeled her inside. "She gets this way sometimes now," he said quietly to Jacqueline who attended her into a back room where she was put to bed for a while, not laughing now, but saying, "Oh, oh," as though she could not get her breath. Esther came down too, and Lawson watched the two women going in and out of the room and then they went upstairs again.

He went into the dining room. No one was there. He wandered into the study, and James was standing by a window, half-asleep on his feet. He jumped when he heard Lawson and began dusting at the window seat. Finally Lawson stood at the bottom of the stairs. There was only one way.

If he could have closed his eyes and done it, he would have. He rushed as though charging an enemy's position, took the stairs two at a time, was onto the landing, breathless, but ran ahead, past his own room and his parents', down the long wing toward the inevitable door and just as he was about to hurtle against it, as though all day he had been falling down the shaft of the landing to this last barrier, the door opened, his mother was there, her eyes wide, and because he could not stop, they collided.

"Oh." She was more surprised than hurt, her arms clinging tightly to him to keep her balance.

"Leggo." He could not see around her.

"Lawson, what in the world?"

"Let me go," and he struggled but he was too out of breath and startled.

For a moment he saw into a room filled with boxes and tissue paper, the end of a rumpled bed, Aunt Esther kneeling with needles in her mouth in front of a half-clothed wire mannequin, Mabel Chipley's square face reflected in a mirror, and then he heard laughing, the two girls, Nora and Bonnie, and he could make out her voice, giggling like a small girl in mischief. His mother closed the door before he could free himself.

"Lawson Wright," and she shook him by the shoulder. "Whatever in the world are you doing here? You can't go in. They're dressing in there."

He could not answer. Even through the door he could hear her laughing, the silence, then bursts of high giggling again.

"Leave me alone."

"What is it, what is it?" his mother insisted as he wrenched away and ran through the hall, down the stairs, out the porch to the driveway, the field, stumbling at last to lie breathless near the grazing herd of cows. For a while he thought he would not get enough air. Then his lungs stopped aching, the coarse grass pricked his neck and arms, and nearby he could hear the heavy tread of cattle and their tearing at the weeds. So it did not matter to her. She was perfectly happy. He had not seen her all day because she had never once thought of him. It was all nothing to her. Nothing at all.

He knew the incident would not pass that easily and he was right. Before dinner his father took him to his room and tried to find out what was wrong. He began sternly, but Lawson could tell his heart was not really in it. He looked very hot and tired. Finally he put a hand on Lawson's knee and stared at him, and Lawson knew he wasn't even thinking about him.

"Look," Bailey said as they started downstairs, "I don't know what this is all about, but do try to steer clear of your mother for a while, won't you? All this fuss gets her so nervous."

He put a hand on Lawson's head and he nodded under it. They went to dinner. Bonnie did not come down, but now Lawson was almost relieved. Edward was late. He was putting on his jacket when he came into the room. "I walked too far," and he looked sheepish. "It took me longer than I expected coming back." As he tucked a napkin into his vest he added, "I scarcely knew the house when I returned," and this led Brody to a long description of the day's events.

After dinner they all went out on the porch for drinks and Mrs. Hutter came by. She was skinny and stiff as a single bone, and mostly sat in silence, her thin face cocked to one side as though listening to every scrap of conversation with intense surprise. "Oh, really?" she said all the time.

Somehow the work had been finished. The tent was tight and secure as a sail full of steady wind. The long tables were decorated with rolls of crepe strips. They all admired it from the porch, were excited, eager as children, and they drank too much.

"Nora's going to stay the night," Lawson heard Aunt Esther say. "I swear I can't pry those two apart for a minute. You'd think they hadn't seen each other for years. Talk, talk, talk," and then she launched into a long description of her own wedding and of how she and Mabel Chipley had been just like that.

After a while Aunt Sally May and Mabel drove away together under the dignified guidance of Marshall and then for a long time they talked about how durable the old lady was and they speculated on her age. Brody insisted he was correct. Lawson tired of their voices. He walked out to the oak, but that was too painful a place to be. Coming back he stopped by the hole in the lawn. The man had not returned to fill it. In the dusk Lawson could not clearly see the bottom. He kneeled by the edge. The sides were sheer, damp earth, smoothed and scarred in places by the mark of the shovel. For a while he dropped small clods of turf that came loose in his fingers. He could hear the voices from the porch and when he looked carefully their white shirts and light dresses pricked out of the dark. He lay full-length with his head over the edge and by shielding his eyes with his hands could see the bottom, part earth and part old boards where the top of the septic tank was. Shaped and gleaming dully, something lay at the far end of the pit as though half-buried and emerging from the soil. He looked away and then back, trying to make out what it could be, but it assumed whatever shape he made in his mind—an old helmet, the top of a chest, a smooth stone, and finally bone, at first the knuckle of a huge joint, but then, in its shadows and markings, a skull—pitted eyes, frail and jagged nose, a mouth where the jaw hung open. He shivered, looked up to where the sky was still white, pocked once by the first star. But when he looked back, he could see nothing in the hole but a skull and his eyes smarted with strain. He did not want to go down, but he could not stop himself. To go away, to never know for sure what it was and perhaps to have it stuck in his dreams, seemed worse.

He looked over to the porch. Aunt Esther was laughing girlishly, as she often did when she was tired. He grasped the edge where some roots had been cut and carefully scrambled over, kicking his toes into the mud. When the roots broke, he dropped quickly, landing with his feet sinking up to the ankles in the muck. He was surprised how deep the hole was. At first he could see nothing clearly. The air was foul. He blinked, keeping his hand, palm flat, against the side, and then he stepped onto the boards beside him, trying to see the object, but there seemed to be nothing there now but the dark, like a black pool of water. Then he heard his own breathing between the walls of earth and no sound of the world outside came down to him. More stars were out, hazy and blurred as though caught in a gray gauze.

When he moved the board turned slightly and made a hollow sound. He held still, aware for the first time that he was on the outer shell of some deeper hole. What if the boards were rotted, or if there was a gap he could not see beyond him? He imagined an endless hollow, rank and dark, narrowing like a funnel where he would be wedged, unable to move in all that stench. He remembered the accounts in newspapers recently of a four-year-old girl who had fallen in an old well; she perched by the water's edge in the dark for days while they tunneled for her, but they could not reach her and they heard her crying once two weeks later and then the sides caved in. But they would never find him. No one knew he was here. He wanted to call out but for a moment he could not breathe. He heard his own heart pounding now like a fist beating against the wet earth.

He tried to move forward. The board bent under him. He knelt, groping with his hand, but the wood seemed firm and without holes. When he reached the end, he crawled onto the earth beyond, even though there was a puddle there that soaked his pants and rose over his wrists. Then he held perfectly still. He had seen something move beneath him, a black rounded shadow like a hooded head, and tiny sparks of light surrounded it. Again it moved, seeming to spread and grow nearer, snuffing the lights.

Even when Lawson saw that it was his own shadow and the sky reflected in the water, the fear did not leave him. The image matched some dream, held him still and tight as though he were coming back again to something he had seen and done before.

He only wanted to get out. He tried to climb the walls but the earth would not hold. He slipped and tumbled, threw himself against the sides and leaped at the brim, but his hands found nothing to hold onto. Once he fell against the boards and bruised his arm, but he did not feel the pain until afterward when he saw there was no way out, when he even stopped yelling and stood with his back to the earth, his eyes closed. After a while the fear was gone. He would have preferred to be afraid. Instead there was a blankness and that beat-beat of his heart. He was numb, fallen somewhere deep inside himself. He couldn't even smell the air anymore. He looked at the stars. They were clear now. He sat down and stared at them until his eyes ached.

When his father called down to him he did not answer at first. That was his father's voice, but the figure was that hooded shadow again, only this time above him. When he answered Brody appeared too. They put the ladder down and he climbed up into the beams of their flashlights.

"Here he is, here he is," Brody kept saying to everyone as they gathered around.

"Lawson Wright, what were you doing? We've been all over looking for you," and his mother was almost hysterical.

He told them nothing about it. He pretended he was hiding. They took out their panic in anger at him—for his sullenness, for his muddy clothes. He pitted himself against them, as though they had kept him from Bonnie and hated him because he loved her, and he would not let them see his fear or anything he had suffered. They did not care anyway. All they cared about were his clothes, the hole (Brody was angry because he had stomped down the sides and made it a bigger mess), their own concern. He turned his face away when his mother came to kiss him.

"I just don't understand," he heard her saying to his father in the hall and when he came in Lawson closed his eyes because in the dark of the bedroom for a moment he did not see his father's features but the black figure again.

When Bailey touched his forehead, Lawson weakened. He wanted to clasp that hand with both of his as though it were the last end of a rope reaching down to him, but his arms felt walled in to his sides. Instead he heard his own voice say dully, "Good night." Then his father was gone. The door shut. He stared at the window, waiting for the moon to come.

7

Lawson stood in the middle of the lawn, surrounded by the wedding guests, watching a curtain billow out through a window on the second story and then collapse against the side of the house. Not too far behind him his father's voice was carried up by the wind. The words were indistinct and ended in a laugh that sounded forced. Lawson turned, saw his father talking to Aunt Fanny, and when she caught sight of him and waved, her skinny hand fluttered like the end of her scarf. His father turned and Lawson could see Fanny forming his own name with her lips. He walked down to them, feeling awkward because of the stiff shirt and the tie that pushed at his throat.

"Well, you'll never see a wedding like this again, Lawson," Fanny said.

"I hope," Bailey added.

Lawson wanted Fanny to go away, for all of them to disappear, and thrashed about to find some way to catch his father's attention.

She was saying, "But it's like us, isn't it? We always try to do too much at the same time. It gets all tangled up."

Lawson clutched his father's arm. A flight of small birds passed far overhead. Someone down the field was calling "Bailey."

"Dad."

His father frowned slightly as though trying to see him clearly.

"What is it?"

Fanny said, "Brody's calling you, Bailey. I think the minister's come."

"What do you want, Lawson?"

"Please don't go now."

"Go? What're you talking about? Come on, son, the wedding's about to begin. Brody's calling."

"Wait."

Bailey raised his arm loose and put it gently around Lawson's shoulders, pulling him against his side. But it made Lawson tense. He wanted to see his father's face.

"Come on," and Bailey began walking him down to Brody who was talking long before they got into hearing distance.

". . . and the minister's here and Charlie hasn't even changed yet and what are we going to do after the wedding if that caterer doesn't get here, for God's sake . . ."

He did not reach an end to his sentence but smothered it with the wadded handkerchief he was passing over his face, came out from behind the white cloth, face pounding scarlet, but dry now, his eyes blinking, and he would have gone on but Bailey started laughing so he stopped with his mouth open, then started laughing also in great choking booms. He slapped Bailey's shoulder hard, stooped slightly toward Lawson, then began to wipe at his brow with the handkerchief again, soothing himself.

"Isn't this the wedding to beat all?" He paused to catch his breath. "Say, I hear old Proctor warming up the organ."

His father began to tap lightly on Lawson's shoulder in time to the music that swelled faintly out of the tent below them. Suddenly Esther was calling Brody from the porch. "Now what," he muttered and walked in long strides up the slope, his buttoned jacket riding up over his hips.

For a few moments they stood there. Since the music had started a number of people drifted off toward the tent, and the lawn began to clear. It had the trampled and abandoned look of a closing carnival. Lawson remembered the day they had gone to the State Fair. He had lost hold of his helium balloon, which drifted up over the trees where its string finally caught and it tugged in the wind. His father had bought him another and he tied it to his wrist this time, but Lawson liked the first one better. He could see it from the place where their car was parked, a small green dot like a mistake in the perfectly blue sky, and it was still there two days later when they drove by the closed fairgrounds.

"Come on, son, let's try to find your mother."

Bailey started to move away, and Lawson could tell by the kind of pat he gave him that he intended to remove his hand. He reached up with both hands and grasping his father's wrist, felt as though he were carrying something over his shoulder that was almost slipping out of his grasp.

"Lawson, what's on your mind?"

He could not look directly at his father but stared at the tables.

"Here." Bailey stooped and Lawson felt a hand on his chin, firmly turning his face until they were looking directly at each other. "Tell me, boy."

"When are we going home?"

"Home? Don't you like it here?"

He shook his head once.

"I know it hasn't been much fun for you, with all the fuss. But after today things will be better. We'll go fishing soon, like I promised. You see, son, it's just that Brody and Esther would like us to stay on for a while, and it's my home too."

Lawson nodded. But he hated to let it go at that. He had not talked with his father for so long. Even now the man seemed to be thinking of something else and was watching everything going on at the same time out of the corners of his eyes.

"Now, come on. I can see your mother down there, and she looks impatient."

She was. When they reached her she glared at them both. "Esther's almost beside herself. She's gone in. Where were you two?"

But since she did not seem to need an answer, they were both silent, and they walked into the opaque, still air of the green tent. Many of the people turned to watch the three of them come up the aisle, and they had to walk all the way to the front row where Aunt Esther was waiting for them.

"Where were you all?" and her whisper carried. "Leave a seat for Brody." She urged them past her to the three vacant chairs.

Lawson found himself between her and his father. She was murmuring something over his head when the organ began again. It was hidden behind a folding screen at one side of the tent, but Lawson could see the player's feet, dark shoes and white socks pumping the air into the small console. Blink, blink went the socks, and when he listened hard he could hear the bellows breathing through the music. Lawson looked around at the other people cautiously. Sitting here in the orderly rows of chairs, with quiet, self-conscious poses, they seemed much more formal and sober than they had outside on the lawn. Directly in front of them at the head of the aisle was a small table spread with a white and gold cloth and on it were a cross and two vases of white flowers. Esther fidgeted with the strap of her purse, her fingers traveling bead by bead to one end and then reversing to the other. When she dressed up, her hands always seemed large and wide, like a man's.

The minister came out from behind the screen, a Bible in one hand. He was wearing a dark robe that swung like a bell over the tops of his shoes and a white cloth hung in two strips over his front. "Oh," and Esther's hands paused, then began their work twice as fast as before. The minister turned to face them, the book clasped in a V by both hands, and he stared down the aisle. Suddenly the sound of a single voice tumbled out, tight and high at first, like laughter. Esther shifted around with a jerk. It was laughter, unmistakable now. Everyone seemed to follow her lead and turn in their seats.

"Oh, my Lord. It's Sally May. She's having one of her fits again."

Lawson could not actually see her, but far to the rear of the tent the figure of Marshall appeared and disappeared as he stooped and rose again. Lawson stood quickly. He could see back over the heads to the bright doorway. Marshall had turned the wheelchair and was starting toward the door where figures of the bridal party were beginning to gather. Then a firm hand on his arm pulled him back into his chair.

"Here now. Sit down," his father said.

Esther's high, thin whisper said, "Oh, can't anything go right?" and his mother reached across Lawson and Bailey to touch her hand. But the laughing was already gone.

Charlie Hutter and his best man paced by slowly to stand at right angles to the minister, and they both looked very thin and serious. The organ began to play more loudly. Lawson sat still. Suddenly the men were looking at something behind Lawson, and Charlie grinned slyly. Lawson did not turn, tense in the back of his neck as though a long wave were reaching up toward him. The bridesmaids passed with Nora holding a tight bouquet. Then he saw Bonnie. She was walking slowly and stiffly on her father's arm, only a small part of her face in view, but it was as composed as a statue's. Brody's eyes shifted about and settled on nothing in particular. The father and daughter stood in front of the minister with the maids fanned out to the sides. As though the organ held only enough music to get them there, it stopped rasping. Esther struggled to unclasp her narrow, rhinestoned purse. She drew out a handkerchief, held it ready in her hand as though she felt a sneeze coming on, and clasped the purse shut.

The service moved too fast for Lawson to follow it. Brody came back to their row and sat down in the empty chair. Esther's hand fluttered over to touch his sleeve and then returned to her lap. Charlie and Bonnie were standing next to each other now with their backs to all of them. Lawson decided that white, stiff figure, veiled and satined, could not be Bonnie, and when she began to repeat her vows, he wondered if a mistake had been made. Surely that voice, clear-toned, high but totally without expression, was not Bonnie's. But when she murmured, "I do," he knew it was her, his heart leaped once like a hooked fish, Esther's handkerchiefed hand rose and even his father shifted his feet quickly as if to stand. Lawson saw them turn to kiss, the music boomed out again, and then they walked past, silently, half-smiling, walking as though afraid that the hummocked ground beneath them would trip them up.

There was nothing left but the empty altar, the screen, and steady pumping glimpse of feet. Esther was holding Brody's hand so tightly that her knuckles showed white. Someone came to escort them out, and for the first time Lawson noticed Mrs. Hutter across the aisle. She too was taken out. There was a short silence. Lawson looked at his father. He was staring at the altar, frowning slightly, his lips pursed. Married, Lawson said to himself, and the word opened and closed in his head like a fan.

When they finally made their way out into the bright spring day, the guests were filling the lawn again in clumps, the bridal party had gathered in a line at the near end of the tables, and people were passing along, shaking hands, kissing. Everyone seemed eager to laugh and talk loudly.

His mother was stopped by some woman who wanted to say again and again how beautiful Bonnie looked.

"Come on," and his father urged him forward. "We've got to congratulate the bride."

The wind began to blow now in quick, violent gusts as if to test the strength of everything standing. In the woods spreading below it was blowing random patches to a lighter green. He and Bailey came up and stood behind the three or four people in line. Lawson could hear Bonnie's voice. He started to walk away.

"Hey," and his father made him turn. "Where are you going?"

"To find Mother."

"She'll be along."

Some people behind them had stopped talking and were watching. Lawson blushed.

"I don't want to."

"Want to what? Come on, Lawson. You always congratulate the bride and groom."

He started to turn away, slowly, that trapped, petulant expression coming over his face even though he was trying to conceal it. He wanted to say something shocking to the people who were watching them. Why couldn't they mind their own business? They made him hesitate and hang there caught between his desire to disobey and the vision of what it would be like to have them see his father chasing him down the field to drag him back to the line. He could tell by his father's tone of voice that he would.

"Come here, Lawson. You hear?"

"Yessir."

He did not look at him, but walked back slowly. Instead he glared at the woman behind them who was smiling at him. He hated that fatuous, gloating expression on her face as though she were about to say, "How cute." He stared until she pursed her lips and turned away to say something to the man beside her. Lawson thought of stepping accidentally on her broad, white-shoed foot, but as soon as he was within reach of his father he was put firmly in front of him. He tried to shrug against the hand but the fingers only tightened.

"Now behave."

They moved forward. Bonnie was partly hidden by the figure of a woman she was embracing, and then there was a gap in the line and he was next. He watched her eyes focus on him, saw the slight hesitation, the little streaks in her mascara where she had been crying, and then she held out her hands to him, smiling.

"Lawson."

He gave her his hand. She was drawing him forward to her. She seemed taller in her white dress and high veil, her mouth was moving uneasily as though the smile would break, and in a moment she would have him close, the other hand already touching his shoulder.

"No," and he wrenched away from her hand so that she was standing there with her arms out. "No."

"Lawson." Because of the loud way he spoke and her tone of voice everyone else in the line looked over.

"No. I hate you." He was hot now, his voice choking up in him.

"Here now," his father boomed. "What are you saying?"

Charlie was standing so stuffed and blank beside her, then through his blurring vision he saw the way she took back her hands and clasped them against her waist, and he started to speak in great sobs that wrenched the words around in his lungs, but already he could feel the strong hand on his arm, yanking him away, propelling him up the lawn. He tried to turn, saw all of them once more standing there and staring, and then as though the gusts of wind that followed them up to the porch had blown them all away, he could see nothing, barely even had to move his stumbling feet because of the way his father nearly carried him up the stairs, into the hall, and over the rugs.

"What the hell, what the hell," the voice over him kept saying and it wasn't until the landing that he began to struggle against the hands that were bruising him with their firm grip.

"Now you get a hold on yourself," and the door slammed behind him.

Lawson hurled himself at the door, kicking and pummeling. After a while he stood completely still. He tried the knob, but the door was locked. He thought about climbing out the window, maybe even of jumping. But when he saw them all standing around on the lawn among the chairs, and green, peaked tent beyond, he turned away. He did not want to be out there. He did not want to be anywhere. Why had they ever come? He went and lay face down on his bed, pressing at the mattress until his own breathing seemed to blow the sheets into white heat.

Bailey walked slowly downstairs and paused on the threshold to the porch. Through the screen he could see the guests, the small knot of wedding party on the lawn. Whatever it was that possessed Lawson was so close to his own feelings that when the dull pounding on the door upstairs suddenly stopped, he felt locked in too. The house and the whole landscape were pressed under the lid of a bright blue box. He turned and strode out through the kitchen, past the startled faces of the help, and out the back, not caring that the dust of the backyard powdered his shoes red, and he kept walking into the fields behind the house, out toward the woods.

He sat against a tree, the house and barn screened from view, his whole body wet with perspiration. Was some kind of madness possessing them all, or was he like a devil in their midst, spreading it out from his own mind? Lawson was so edgy, doing such unaccountable things, and last night he had been incapable of helping his son, had stared down at his face, a pale disk his hand touched, and then he had been afraid, as if that face and anything his hands could reach were fading, sinking back into some place beyond his understanding.

The wedding had been unbearable to him. Sitting alone now, it all seemed very unreal, but out there on the lawn before they had entered the tent, he had felt defensive, as though he wanted to tell the guests that he had nothing to do with the lavish scene. He had tired of shaking hands, flicking out the same words again and again: Yes, it was lucky the weather was so fine, wasn't the tent lovely, beautiful day, lovely tent. But when he looked down the lawn to it he felt nothing but aversion. Finally everyone had been sucked into it and his own mind went blank, letting himself be pulled down into that same hole with the others. Once inside, he had begun to sweat profusely. People were pressing from behind and all their stirrings, their coughs or whispers, broke over him like a wave. Just as quickly he would become calm, remote, as though he had left his body and become a totally unrelated observer. He saw the small patterns on the screen and each note the organ played was clear and separate. Turning quickly he looked at Jacqueline whose face was absorbed in watching the altar, as if she saw something was happening already. When the wedding party stood there he stared at them. They looked perfectly composed and stereotyped, and their bodies became mere pasteboard, as if they had come to a carnival and were sticking their faces over the edge of a painted tableau while some unseen photographer waited to take their picture. The heads were interchangeable. He turned slightly, glanced at the first row beside them and placed their faces over the wedding party's. Then he put Jacqueline's in Bonnie's place, but could not fill in his own, and the body beside her became faceless. Finally as if in a daguerreotype he put himself there, but Nora was the bride, so he gave up the whole game and tried to listen to the words. When the ceremony was over, the couple turned. Bailey thought of their bodies naked, cruelly bare, without the slightest sensuality, models in an anatomy text. Nora walked beside the best man, smiling like an archaic statue, and he could not take his eyes off the white V of her neck and lift of collarbones. He knew she was looking at him but he did not stop staring and then she was past. When he saw how Jacqueline was gazing past him vaguely and had even been crying, he was sure she had been remembering their wedding, and he thought of touching her hand beside him, but didn't. She was so sentimental at weddings. Marriage, he had said to himself, trying to make the word do something to him.

He twisted uncomfortably against the ridged bark. A squirrel was scolding steadily above him. He thought he could hear a burst of voices carried down by the breeze, and he stood slowly to walk back across the field with his jacket hooked over his shoulder. In the kitchen he helped himself to a glass of champagne, put on his jacket, and walked back out to the hallway. No one seemed to have missed him and he mingled with the guests again. "Wasn't it adorable the way Emma Jean caught the bouquet?" Fanny said to him, and he nodded. The champagne helped. But all the time he could not get Lawson out of his mind. He felt him locked in that room as though part of himself were manacled and lying in a narrow trunk. Yet he could not face talking to him. He watched Bonnie moving among the guests, and when she reached him, she took him aside.

"Where's Lawson?"

"In his room." He looked at the toes of her shoes barely showing under the white hem.

"What's wrong? Did he say?"

"Oh, just tired. Excited. Too many people." He could feel her staring hard at him.

"Can I see him?"

Her eyes were unflinching in a face without that smiling mask she usually wore.

"I think you'd better not, Bonnie. I want to talk to him first.

He's pretty worked up," and even as he spoke he wondered if he had betrayed Lawson, knowing the boy probably did want to see her.

She hesitated, then murmured, "All right. But you'll tell him I want to talk to him? Soon."

Bailey nodded, she turned and swayed off through the guests toward the porch. He glanced once up toward the house, guiltily, and started when a hand curled around his arm and Jacqueline said, "Where have you been? I looked all over for you."

As if seeing her for the first time in weeks, he took in that auburn hair drawn back so neat and tight, those high but delicate cheekbones, somehow a perfect setting for the quiet, expressive eyes, and suddenly he wanted to kiss her so he did, quickly on the lips, and she smiled.

"Come on," and she stood very close for a moment while something clenched in him, "they want to have us in the photographs," and she took his hand to walk slowly with him to the porch where the family was waiting.

After a while Lawson began to listen to the guests laughing and talking in a soft babble below, and from the other side of his door, perhaps from a room across the hall, a low, sporadic moaning came, which he finally recognized as the voice of Aunt Sally May, calming herself restlessly. He turned over onto his back. His tie was pleated and crushed, his suit jacket wrinkled, and he knew how his mother would scold him for that almost more than for anything else that had happened. Voices passed quickly in the hallway, and light footfalls. He thought he could hear Nora's voice once. He went to the door and put his ear to it but everything was still again, except for the moaning. Even that was less frequent. When he looked around the room again, he noticed how bare it was and then realized that nothing belonging to Uncle Edward was there. He opened the dresser drawers. They were empty. Had he left already, without even saying good-bye?

He went to the window. Suddenly everyone seemed to be gathering toward the house. A car was coming up the driveway and worked its way through the guests. They were watching the porch. All the young girls were at the edge of the driveway, and Nora was in the front, one hand held lightly to her bare neck. Something flashed out from under the roof, the girls reached and a child in front jumped at the object that settled in the hands of the girl next to Nora, and Lawson could see that it was a bouquet of flowers. Then they all pressed around the girl who had caught it as if they wanted to touch her and some of the people nearby were clapping.

He was afraid they might look up and see him, so for a while he sat in the chair, staring out at the hills and sky. But when the people began yelling again he had to look down at them, and that was when Charlie came running out and around the hood of the car to the driver's side, his head ducked forward, and everyone was throwing something—white, hard particles that bounced like hail off the hood of the car.

He saw Bonnie come from underneath. She went to the side of the car. The door was locked and she was trapped there for a moment, dressed now in a light red suit, and she screamed with one hand held up against the stuff they threw, so thick that it gathered in her hair like snow. Lawson pressed his hand against the window. She was laughing as much as she was screaming and he could hear her say, "Charlie, Charlie, oh, oh." The door swung open, she climbed in, the door shut, he could see her face as she turned, grinning, to push down the lock, and the car began to move, slowly because the people did not stand aside. The car turned around the half circle, started downhill, gathered momentum, and sped toward the highway, dragging a few lines of tin cans that leaped and smashed in its wake. As the car went away from him, Lawson felt something attached to his chest being pulled thinner and thinner until when the car turned out of sight the band seemed to snap back against him, leaving a hollowed-out pain. "Bonnie," he said once with both hands on the window, and then afraid that someone would see him, he walked back to sit on the edge of his bed.

He was not sure how long he had been sitting there. Edward's clock had always been on the bureau, but now it was gone. Lawson heard cars coming and going, and once two men passed down the hall and then returned. They were talking in firm undertones and one of them laughed, but Lawson could not tell who they were. When everything seemed to be quieting down, he heard a click against the door and saw the knob revolve. There was a light tap.

"Lawson?"

It was Edward's voice, and he jumped from the bed, tried the knob, but the door was still locked.

"Can't you come in? Can't you let me out?"

"The key isn't here. I guess they took it away."

Lawson pressed the side of his face against the crack in the door. He remembered a movie he had once seen of a man locked inside a glass shower stall with the water rising slowly.

"I can't anyway, Lawson. It's not my business to. I'm going now. James is taking me down to the bus station. I wanted to say . . ."

"But what shall I do?"

There was a long silence from the other side of the door. Lawson could hear neither breathing nor footsteps. Finally he could not stand hanging like that over the long pause. "Uncle Edward?"

"Yes. I'm here."

But Lawson was angry. What did it matter if he was there? He could do nothing. He was only crazy Uncle Edward going back to Richmond and could not even get him out of a locked room. Why couldn't the man at least come in? He wanted to touch Edward, to put his head against that bulging, brocaded vest instead of this hard and solid door.

"I'll have to go. Good-bye for now, Lawson."

No motion, then a kind of muffled tread, the creak of a carpeted floorboard.

"Uncle Edward?" he said tentatively, but there was no answer. "Uncle Edward?" he tried more loudly.

He ran to the window. In a few minutes he saw the man come out, stoop into a car, and the door was closed by Aunt Esther. A few guests were still standing on the lawn, but most of them had left. Lawson pushed at the window, but it was stuck. The car drove off and Lawson backed away until he could feel the edge of the bed behind and he sat down. It wasn't fair. They were all going away. He imagined everyone leaving and himself still there in the locked and empty house. He turned down the covers and climbed into bed with his clothes and shoes still on. He was shivering and could not seem to get warm enough.

When his father came Lawson was dozing. The room had fallen slightly away from him, assuming strange shapes. Sometimes it became his own room in Richmond, then turning and spinning in his hooded eyes it became a room he had never seen before, bare of furniture and with wide, fluted columns at one end. There were never any people where he went. The room narrowed to a corridor. When he looked back he could see nothing and the walls were pinching together like a tube of toothpaste. He was beginning to be frightened when he saw the corridor become the one-armed rocking chair in the corner with his suitcase standing beside it and felt a hand gently kneading his shoulder.

"Lawson? Are you awake, son?"

He opened his eyes wide, held perfectly still, felt himself turn rigid as though he had been poured to cool in the shape his sleeping body had taken. His father was sitting on the bed, and he let go of Lawson's shoulder to lean on his outstretched arm. Lawson was surprised. He had expected something he could strike out against or resist, but his father did not seem angry at all. With the late afternoon sun shining behind him, his face was hard to see clearly, but Lawson recognized the hesitant curve of the lips as though the man were about to say something sad but had decided not to. From somewhere in the field and surprisingly close came the sporadic dull thump of a cow bell.

"They've all gone, haven't they?" Lawson said.

His father nodded. "Yes. They've all gone."

"Even Aunt Sally May?"

"Even her."

He knew he did not really care, but he began crying.

"She's going to die, isn't she?"

Bailey brushed at the hair on Lawson's forehead.

"Sally May? What is it, son? Why are you worried about her?"

"I don't care," and he tossed away from his father's hand. "I hope she dies." He stopped crying, and they were both silent. Somewhere two voices began talking on the lawn accompanied by the sound of chairs being slapped flat and stacked.

"Why did you say those things to your cousin?"

"Because it's the truth. Because I hate her."

But having said it, Lawson rose, the covers tangled against him and pulling him back, but he clung to his father who held him close to the suit that smelled now of sweat, cigar smoke, and that sweet, slightly rotten odor he knew was whiskey.

"Tell me," Bailey said. "You can tell me."

He did. For a while he clung to him, hearing the sound of his father's slow breathing, the way his words seemed to come out of his chest, and the distant pulse. Then he began brokenly. Throughout all of it he kept swearing his father to secrecy, although he was not sure who else there was to keep it all from, and there wasn't much to tell.

When Bailey said, "We won't tell your mother, Lawson. She wouldn't understand. Not right away," it seemed so far away from what he wanted. "OK?" his father asked.

"Yes," and Lawson felt that by agreeing he had only closed

something off again. He wanted to know why she would not understand, and other questions were waiting to come out after that, but he let it go. Instead he confessed to being afraid, to not liking the dark of this room and of waking to see a hooded man in the light of the window.

A blue jay fluttered to rest on the window ledge, craned and twisted his peaked head as though following intricate movements below him, then dropped out of sight.

"Lawson," and Bailey put one hand flat on his chest as though trying to hold him down and at some distance, "I can't really tell you much about all that. You must try not to be afraid of the dark. There is nothing here that will hurt you on purpose. We all love you and are looking out for you." He paused, lifted his hand, and put it on his own knee. "It's just being brave that counts, Lawson. You have to have courage. We all do."

When Esther began calling them, Bailey stood quickly and pulled back the covers.

"Come on. It's time for dinner."

Lawson hesitated, afraid to go down and face them all. But his father waited at the door.

All evening everyone acted as if nothing much had happened. Only his mother seemed a little angry still, but Aunt Esther told so many funny stories about the wedding that after dinner they all entered a slap-happy and exhausted state. His uncle took him out to the barn where the cows were being milked. Then they all sat on the porch late into the night, which ended when Lawson became vaguely aware that someone was carrying him up what seemed to be an endless flight of stairs.

8

Bailey was surprised how quickly everything was dismantled. The lawn was mashed and rutted, and Brody said it would be a year before the grass looked right again, but Esther said she didn't mind, it had been just perfect. As things settled down, Bailey began to wonder whether he should have committed himself to staying for two months. He had to find some means of getting away from Brody for periods of time.

What he began to find amusing were his late afternoon appointments tutoring Nora. He would be waiting for her in Brody's study, or if he was late she would be at the desk, perched on her elbows over the opened text. She was more responsive than he had expected, even if not very bright. In one week they had moved quickly through five lessons in her text, and she was certain that she had never understood so well. With the problems out of the way, there always seemed to be time to talk, and she was a very good listener, leaning forward over the sheet of paper they used in common, asking questions, fascinated. He was flattered. By the second week he found himself telling her about all sorts of things. They talked about the wedding and then about Bonnie. Did he think she would be happy?

He smiled. "For a while."

"What do you mean?"

"Oh, the beginning's easy. It's after four or five years that it really begins."

She shook her head. "I don't think I'll ever get married."

Sometimes she repeated herself like that, forgetting previous conversations, but he did not mind.

"I just can't see it," and she tossed her head as if hair were in her eyes. "I mean staying with one person for so long."

He laughed. "It sounds like you move around."

"I have friends," and then as if that bored her, "How long have you been married?"

But all he said was, "Long enough," and turned the page to the next lesson.

Soon she opened up and began talking about Billy and how hard it was to be some kind of mother to him since theirs was dead. For the first time Bailey was truly sorry for her. She was older than she let herself appear. He did not know what to say. Suddenly she was crying and put her head down on her arms. "I'm sorry," she said in a muffled voice. Bailey never knew what to do with women who cried. He looked at the bowbend of her slender back, the tanned flesh where her blouse had risen out of her shorts, the way her legs were tucked under the folding chair and the sandals hung loosely away from her heels, then reached out and put his hand gently on the back of her neck, stroking lightly. She did not move. "I'm sure everything will be all right," he said ineptly, and after a while she sat up smiling, wiping her eyes and apologizing until he reached out to touch one finger to her lips. She put her head down again, and this time Bailey moved his hand up and down her back. She turned her face on its side, smiling, her eyes closed.

"That feels good," she murmured.

After she had driven away, he stood on the porch and chided himself. Was this some second adolescence? But he wasn't going to stop. This wouldn't go much further. No harm in being a little foolish, especially when you could still make fun of yourself. Besides, it was somehow exciting, giving him something new to think about, and he was completely in control, knew where he was going.

Once he met her downtown in the morning and she drove him home, the top down, her hair flying back, and when she honked at a group of her friends gathered by the dairy bar, he could not help staring back at them, trying to look at ease. That was too much. What was he doing? Next he would be driving with her up to some hot dog stand where they would be surrounded by those louts self-consciously fingering their cigarettes. When they reached the house he said, "I will see you later this afternoon," and tried to be very formal, but she did not seem to catch that in his voice. He watched as her red and chrome car blazed into the dust she had raised in coming. So be it, he said as he walked toward the barn. That kind of junk he didn't have to take, but he could take her. What he only let himself acknowledge briefly was that she was on his mind almost all the time now.

He walked down after lunch to the beach where he knew she would be, reached the end of the bridle path, and saw her lying there, sunning with her eyes closed, her straps loosened and tucked out of sight, and she leaned up on one elbow and put a hand over her eyes.

"Hello."

"No wonder you've got such a tan."

She pulled at the top of her suit. He stood there for a while and talked with her describing something Uncle Eustace had done once. It came to him very vividly how Uncle Eustace had been so free and gay and prankish. After all, wasn't that what made him so appealing, his spontaneity, the way he could say and do things that all the adults wanted to say and do but would not let themselves? That was why the children liked him most of all.

Bailey took off his shoes and socks, rolled up his pants, and stood almost up to his knees in the water.

"I wish I'd thought to bring my suit."

Nora, leaning on her elbows, her body angling toward him, smiled. "It's hot, isn't it?"

He stepped in a little deeper so that the water lapped against the rolled cuffs. Minnows nipped tentatively at his ankles.

"It's tempting," and he moved back, felt his foot going deeper than it should, staggered, and then found himself crouching in the water. He got up slowly, she was laughing, and as soon as the shock of it left him, he began laughing too.

"Well," and he came out to drip on the sand, "I guess I'm going in anyway."

He did not care. The cool water felt fine. He stripped to his shorts.

"I'll be back in a minute," and he ran down until the water was deep enough to catch his legs and throw him forward and he dove, swimming under the water, eyes open in the murk until he had to come up, breathless, and he swam with long, easy strokes, then lay on his back to catch his wind. He floated there, his face and chest warmed by the sun, eyes veiled by the bright blood of his eyelids, the chill water under him falling away to places where dark currents were passing back and forth. Hell, what did anything matter but just feeling your body alive like this, and turning onto his belly, he began swimming slowly back to the beach.

She lay as though sleeping, but her hands were smoothing the sand. He walked up quietly and stepped between her and the sun, letting water drip onto her.

"Oh," and she leaned up again.

He laughed, abruptly, and kneeled beside her, his hands on her thighs. She took off her glasses and looked at him with a puzzled smile.

"I'm going to kiss you." He leaned forward, his arms straddling her.

She did not move. When he kissed her she flinched slightly.

The next time she closed her eyes. He bent forward, harder, put his tongue against her lips, tasting their salt, and suddenly her mouth was open. Her hands tensed on his back, he took in the smell of her, and when he thrust one leg between her thighs they parted and she moved her body against him.

"What are you doing?" she said, but he knew she was not asking him to stop.

He stood and pulled her to her feet, took her hand and led her back into the woods, and at the first tangle of honeysuckle away from the path, he helped her take off her bathing suit. Then they lay down on the matted leaves and vines. When she said his name, "Bailey, Bailey," he almost laughed, as though calling him by his first name were more intimate than anything else.

When he went to bring his clothes from the beach, he walked quickly into the open and then back to where she lay curled on her side. They were close to the trail and anyone on the opposite shore could have seen them on the beach. But when he lay beside her again they were hidden. He had brought her bag back and she took a cigarette from it, which he lit, noticing how her hands trembled, and as she sucked in the flame she looked at him. They did not talk much and shared the cigarette. When she said, "Isn't it strange?" he only nodded, stroking her face with his hand, closely fingering those flat, tilted cheeks as if eager to touch what his eyes had stared at for weeks. "It's all right, it's all right," he soothed, and she did not hold back when he pulled her to him again.

Finally she dressed and combed her hair to gather it in a neat tail. They set a time to meet the next day at the same place, and she stooped to kiss him before she left, arms very taut around his neck, and then she was gone. He dressed in the trousers that were still damp, and then lay down again on his back in the vines, hands under his head. He couldn't believe how new and strange it was to have the smell and touch of a different woman on him, as though he had been walled away from them for years. In the late afternoon he woke and walked slowly back through the woods and fields.

Even as he passed the barn he wavered between extremes: a moment when everything seemed new and open, and then a terrible blankness when he was certain he could never feel anything again and the house before him paled like a negative exposed to sunlight. He wondered if this was guilt. But that evening as he went through the usual motions of taking a shower before supper, putting on a fresh shirt that smelled slightly of the kitchen and of Emily's hands, he was exhilarated, as though their meetings, the shared secret and the way it would fill some days to come, were a fixed point to hold onto. He drank too much before dinner, knew he was speaking too often and laughing too loudly, but everyone seemed to enjoy it, and Brody put his hand on his brother's shoulder as they went out to sit on the porch with their cigars and bourbon after dinner. Bailey even leaned forward to Brody, who was easing back in the chair as though he could retreat from his overstuffed insides, and poked him quickly with one finger in the gut, making him jump and spill some of his drink. But something was wrong with the women. Esther was so silent, and instead of being in the center of the conversation, she would lapse in and out, staring off down the driveway with an expressionless face. In spite of the fact that he knew she could not know what he had done, her mood made him uneasy. Did she have some intuition?

Jacqueline was edgy too and shrugged off his hand at one point when he rested it on her shoulder at dinner. He took it for one of her moods, the way she often became remote and demure when he felt most exuberant. But he sensed all evening that she wanted to talk to him, and that when they would be alone he would have to face her. He tried to fill out the evening. Lawson was allowed to stay up later than usual and went out to the barn where he was making something with scraps of lumber and tools lent him by Brody. Bailey kept them all sitting out on the porch well past ten o'clock until even Brody began to yawn and fall silent.

Upstairs at last and alone with her, Bailey washed and undressed as quickly as possible and then made himself appear absorbed in reading the book he plucked from the bedside table. She took much too long brushing her hair and he could tell that often she paused to look beside herself in the mirror and stare at his reflection. He was propped in the bed, turning pages, but the words were inked blurs. If she would only turn out the lights and quietly fall to sleep in her usual stubborn silence.

"Bailey."

"Um?" He had reached the end of a chapter. He concentrated on the title of the next, desperately.

"Bailey, can't you put that book down? For just a moment. I want to talk to you. Please."

He looked up to see her reflected face staring back at him, the brush held upright in her fist on the table.

"What's the trouble?"

She did not answer. He looked away, found an envelope on the bedside table, and put it between the pages where he had stopped.

"Bailey, we have to talk."

"What about?"

"I'm not sure. We haven't spoken more than a few words for weeks, it seems to me. What's wrong?"

Her voice caught. She turned from the mirror so that she was facing him, her velvet shawl slightly awry. He noticed how thin she looked, how her collarbones thrust out from the pale skin.

"There's nothing wrong, is there?"

"I don't know. You're so quiet. So distant. You never look at me even, or touch me. And all day long you wander about as though . . ."

"As though what?"

"Don't you know what I mean? Don't you even feel it? I talk, talk, talk with Esther, we spend our days gabbling for hours, and even Lawson stays by himself as though he's sick of everyone. Oh, I know you must be worried about your job, and it must be hard on you to be with Brody when he's so, so . . ." Again she stopped, this time looking down into her lap where the brush lay. "Tell me, though. Tell me about it."

He pushed himself up against the headboard. It bothered him to be able to see his own face beyond her in the mirror, and so he sat up until he became a headless figure bound in white sheets to the waist.

"There's nothing to tell, really. I'm just tired, and as you say, worried. Aren't you having a good time?"

She looked at him once then stood abruptly with her back to him, loosening the ties of her dressing gown.

"Never mind."

"What do you mean 'never mind'? You don't have to act as though I insulted you."

"You know what I mean. I don't want to play games. I thought you might go a little further than 'good night' and 'good morning,' I thought maybe . . ." but she ended that sentence by tossing the velvet in a rumpled heap on the chair and turning to her bed where she peeled the covers down in a rough, tearing motion.

"Finish your sentences, at least. You want me to talk and you can't even finish your sentences," but he was sorry when he said that, and she, lying straight under the covers, turned stiffly away from him.

For a while they were silent.

"You can turn the light out if you're through reading."

He did. But in the dark, silent because she was not moving and he was breathing so tightly, he felt worse.

"I'm sorry, Jacqueline, it's just that . . ."

"It doesn't matter."

Her words at first stung him like a slap in the face, but when he heard the suffering in them, the way the last word ended high, on the verge of tears, he pulled back the covers and came to her bed. At first she did not move. He gently lifted the sheet and its thin blanket and slid down into the bed beside her, placing his body against her curled back, letting his leg ride up to rest on her thigh. He ran one hand along her hip, past the jutting bone and up the ribs until her breast was cupped in his palm. At first she did not move, barely breathing. Then she turned, a slow pivot of her body until they lay face to face on their sides.

"Oh, Bailey, Bailey. I'm so lonely."

But he did not want to hear her words. He put one hand on her face, stopping her lips gently, and then he kissed her and lifted the nightgown. She pulled him onto her and held him tightly, saying his name as though it could keep him there forever.

Later he lay still on her as she breathed against his weight, and he felt dizzy, almost sick, and the room was black gauze around him. He rolled onto his side again while she held one arm tightly around his neck.

"Bailey, please, can't we go home? You and Lawson and I, couldn't we go home again, this place . . ."

He jerked free of her arm, then stayed propped on his elbows, her face now leaning against his forearm. She found his hand with both of hers and held it.

"Home? You know this is home for me. Besides the idea of Richmond right now, the heat and nothing to do, and I'm sure Lawson . . ."

"Lawson? Do you really think of Lawson? Or of me either? Can't you see us both, Bailey? He wanders around all day, and I know he's into all sorts of trouble, and I'll say it anyway, but we might as well be home and you working for all the time you spend with him."

She said it all quietly, not with the bitterness he had expected. It was true, they ought to go home.

"We can't go back to Richmond. Not yet."

"Why, Bailey? Tell me why? Can't you give me that much?"

"I don't know."

He took his hand away from hers, not roughly, but she let go unwillingly, and he swung his feet out onto the floor to sit there on the edge of the bed. For a moment the idea came to him that she should know, that if he could tell her everything, now, it would not be too late, and there would be a kind of resurrection in it too, pouring out all the strange and half-mad, tilted days, the obsession of memories and his senses and that bare-hipped girl in the wood. But his tongue was like a stone that would not roll back. She said nothing else. He stood up at last and went back to his bed. As he was rolling slowly into sleep, his body aching and tired as though its strength had been drained out from the groin, he thought he heard weeping and as though his own voice were speaking, he heard his mind say, "She is crying, I think."

Bailey rose early. If Jacqueline woke, she did not show it, and he dressed quietly, not pausing to shave. He tiptoed down the stairs. Lately these early mornings, when some dew was still on the lawn, and no one else was up, were the best times of day for him, and he could, for an hour or so, forget everything, his mind suspended like the nearly stationary, new sun. He reached the hallway when he heard a slight sound in the darkly curtained living room and he paused. Someone was standing there in a bathrobe. Esther, her back turned, and she was quietly weeping. He couldn't move, and the sight of that unknown grief coming so suddenly scared him. Finally she half turned, saw him, and said, "Oh, dear."

He walked up to her and put a hand on her shoulder. She had a handkerchief in her hand, which she was prodding her nose with. Her face, puffed and weary, looked so much older.

"What's wrong, Esther?"

He had never seen her weep before, had never even imagined it, and the confused, helpless face did not seem to belong to her.

"I'm sorry, Bailey, dear. I didn't think anyone was up."

"Can I help? Is everything all right?"

She looked at him sheepishly, almost smiled, but then a sob heaved her shoulders against his hand.

"It's nothing, really."

"You're sure?"

She nodded, and then, like a little girl, the words tumbled out, "Oh, it's just my Bonnie, my child, I miss her so, and I know she's only a few miles away, and she's so happy and all, but the house is just empty without her, and sometimes I wake in the middle of the night and listen and get angry thinking, 'That child, that child, hasn't she come home yet?' and then I remember she's not coming home again, this isn't her home anymore," and then her head bent down, the forehead leaning against Bailey's collarbone, and she sobbed.

Bailey put a hand on her shoulder. He was deeply moved but could say nothing. He patted the woman's back until she quieted.

"There, now, you see how silly a mother is?" and she drew back to blow her nose.

"Not at all, not at all," and then he lied because it was all he could think of, "I've missed her too."

"You have? Oh, isn't it awful? She just seems to be in every room I go into these days." She was smiling now. "Well, I'm going to go get dressed. You won't tell Brody on me, will you? He thinks I'm so silly."

Bailey shook his head and watched her sway off toward the stairs, her muffled, unbound figure lumpish over the thick, bare ankles. After she was gone he walked out onto the porch. For just a moment he felt a strange humility and almost wept himself. She hadn't been thinking of him at all last night, but of Bonnie. All of the people around him, Brody, Jacqueline, even Lawson, were suffering things he did not really know about at the time, but somehow he always thought it was connected to himself. It wasn't. Even when he was the cause of the pain, as with Jacqueline, he could not really understand how it felt.

He shook his head, could not decide if what he was thinking was very funny or very lonely. What did seem amusing finally was how many grieving women he had comforted lately. He yawned, standing in the hot, early sun, stretched, then leaned his shoulder against one of the pillars, watching the setter sidle along the path, tongue out and eyes averted. The dog pawed slowly up the steps, tail wagging, sniffed Bailey's shoes, and flopped down beside him, staring out and blinking as though he could feel a hand already caressing his head. Even when Bailey's skin began to prickle and sweat, he did not move. He wanted to be aware of nothing but his body.

9

They were invited to Bonnie's new house for lunch. Lawson did not want to go. He had decided he would never see Bonnie again, and especially with so many other people. But his mother refused to listen to any excuses. Furthermore, he had to wear his suit and a tie, like at the wedding.

The house was new, only one story, and was the first on a road that had just been built. But their lot was bordered by a grove of hickory, and the developers had promised that no houses would be raised behind theirs. Charlie explained all this as he led them around the outside, and Lawson hung back, looking at the new, stunted boxwood and azaleas sitting browned and scruffy in the scarred earth. Bonnie had not come out to greet them, was still dressing, they were told. He kept his eyes turned away from the house. Charlie had a new jacket, its huge blue and maroon checks giving his smile a clownish twist.

"There she is," Jacqueline said, and Lawson could hear them

all kissing behind him, but he stared hard at the little wooden stakes that marked the edge of the property.

"Hello, Lawson," and her voice was by his shoulder.

He looked around and she was standing with one hand on his father's arm, draped in a blue dress that hung nearly to her ankles, looking lost in it and very thin.

" 'Lo," and he stared at the side of her face. But she did not come any nearer or touch him, and they were all talking to her at once.

When they went into the house to be shown around he came too and walked a little behind her, watching her when he knew she could not see him. They stopped for a long time in the kitchen.

"Hey, Lawson." Charlie was beside him, and he put a a big-knuckled hand on his shoulder. "I've seen all this. C'mon and help me set up the croquet."

He didn't care, but he went with him anyway, out into the backyard, which was fresh grass but carefully mown, and sitting by the door was a new croquet set, its stripes bright and shiny.

"Do you play much?" Charlie measured out the distances with careful strides.

"Sure. I guess."

Actually Lawson was good at croquet. There was room in the backyard at home, and he played a mean game, liking nothing better than the moment he could send another ball flying way out of reach. After they had set up the wickets, Charlie left to make some drinks and Lawson knocked a ball around. He liked blue. The ball rolled evenly and fast on the clipped lawn. He watched Nora drive up and was relieved to see she had not brought Billy with her.

After they all had drinks and Charlie had started the charcoal in the barbecue, they divided up into teams, and Lawson was given Nora. He watched her practice a little. She was OK, but not very accurate.

"Here," he said, "lookit. Hold it like this," and he showed her how to get a better grip so she could keep her eye on the ball too. She was being very giggly and kept saying loud things to Bonnie, but she listened seriously to Lawson. Charlie brought him a Coke. Out of the corner of his eyes he watched Bonnie line up her ball and shoot first, and he could tell she was good, but she had Charlie for a partner and he hit the ball so hard that it always veered off to the bushes or the tree trunk and he would say, "Damn," under his breath. Bailey and Esther played together, and Lawson had to keep an eye on Brody because after everyone had finished one drink and started on another, he cheated, just little things like stepping on someone's ball so it mashed into the ground, and when they hit it, the ball would pop out of the hole and go every which way, or he would stand by his ball or Jacqueline's and nudge it with his toe so it was better lined up on the wicket. Everyone thought it was a big joke, but Lawson began to get angry and whenever he caught Brody he would yell, "Hey, Uncle Brody, you quit it," and would stalk back over the lawn to put the ball right again, looking crossly at his innocently smiling uncle. Brody was always taking Jacqueline aside and whispering to her as if they had a strategy, but Lawson knew better than to pay attention because it was just to make everyone nervous. Besides, he had enough to do telling Nora how to play her shots. She turned out to be pretty dumb, although when she made a mistake she thought it was funny, and she would look around, especially at his father, and giggle, and then they would laugh about it, which made Lawson mad because he decided they ought to win easily.

Which they did anyway. He went through the last wickets and came back on everyone, knocking their balls all over the place, and he hit Brody's so hard once that they all had to look for it in the bushes by the edge of the woods, and Nora finally came in safely, so they quit. The only player Lawson was really afraid of was his father because he had seen him go all the way round without stopping a few times back in Richmond, but today he seemed very sloppy and sometimes did not even remember which was his ball. Maybe that was because he had at least three drinks.

They were standing around afterward and Nora was telling him how good he was, when Bonnie came up and listened, and she was staring at him, so he looked back for the first time directly into her eyes. The others were all clustered around the barbecue, talking about something to do with politics, so when she said quietly, "Lawson, can I talk to you for a minute?" he said "OK," and slowly they wandered off across the lawn toward the trees.

For a while she did not say anything, just walking on her bare feet, the blue bell of her dress swinging against her ankles. They reached the edge of the trees, but did not stop until they were on the little path and a screen of tree trunks was between them and the house. Then they stopped and she sat abruptly on the grass, tucking her dress around her legs. She patted the ground.

"Please, sit down."

Lawson did. Back through the trees and shade he could see the lawn and the knot of people, and the house, which seemed very small and low from here.

"I wish you'd tell me what was wrong." She did not look at him, but plucked at some grass.

Suddenly he remembered exactly what it was like again to be standing on the lawn, her hands reaching toward him, but just as quickly he did not feel anger, but a pain, that awful tug in his chest as she drove away. So simply, and because he had said it now so often in his own mind that it did not seem at all strange to him, he said, "I love you."

She held a single blade of grass between her thumb and forefinger, staring at it and turning it slowly.

"Lawson," and she looked at him directly again, "you know I love you very much too."

"But you're married," he blurted. "You love Charlie," and his face blazed, his collar choking at him.

"No, silly. Don't you know you can love lots of people at the same time? There are lots of different ways of loving."

He did not know why but that made him both happy and miserable. He had said he loved her, but she did not seem to understand.

"I wouldn't ever want to hurt you, Lawson. I didn't understand when you yelled at me that way."

His eyes began to sting and he looked away angrily.

"I didn't want to go through that line. They made me."

But she did not answer for a while.

"Lawson, I want to be your friend. I want you to get to know Charlie better. And besides, we've got so much to talk about, so much only we can understand. I think we need each other."

Did she mean all that? He watched her face carefully. She was talking to the ground, to the clump of grass where her hand rested now.

"We're special, you and me. We're the last Wrights, and we're both the only child in our families, and I don't think they understand us very well."

"Who?"

"Them," and her hand swept out to the group that hovered by the back porch. "Even Charlie. Who else can I really talk to? Or you? We need each other."

He listened to her carefully, but he couldn't find any words now. Yet he liked something she was saying, and he tried to memorize it all so he could think about it later.

"C'mon," and she stood, reaching down with her hand. "Won't you forgive me if I did something wrong?"

He took the hand and she pulled, and he came up awkwardly, almost bumping her, and then her hand was on his cheek.

"Dear Lawson," and if he could have, he would have stood like that forever, but she turned and he followed her, and partway across the lawn she smiled and said, "Race you," and before she could start he was off and would have got there first but his foot caught in a wicket and he fell, she jumped over him and reached the house first.

But everyone seemed subdued, and when Bonnie asked where Bailey was, they said he'd suddenly just put down his food and told them he had to go home and left without explaining. They did not talk about that anymore, and Brody tried to be funny and tell some jokes that Charlie laughed at very hard, but Lawson could tell his mother was upset, and Nora left early because she said she had to take Billy to the dentist's. When they reached home James said his father had gone for a walk and would be back for supper. But Lawson did not care much. He had too much to think about.

The next day when Brody suggested fishing, Lawson was evasive. He did not want to fish with Uncle Brody because that was something his father had promised to do with him. But recently at the dinner table when he asked his father he would say, "Soon, Lawson, pretty soon," and Lawson knew what that meant.

"I'm not sure."

Brody flicked his cigar against the railing, which he never did when Esther was there because it made dark smudges.

"Maybe you're too busy."

"It's not that. Dad and I were going fishing soon anyway."

"No harm in fishing more than once."

"I guess."

"I'm going fishing tomorrow morning. I'd love to have you come along."

They watched a high jet make a trail, but no sound reached them.

"They say the bass are biting."

"I might as well," and Lawson tried to hold the corners of his mouth tight when Brody laughed and shook him with the hand he put around his neck.

It was a good day for fishing. At least Brody said so when they shoved the boat out on the lake so early in the morning that all the fog had not burned off, and they rowed sometimes through wisps riding sideways toward them. "Dragon breath," Brody called them. Lawson could remember how when younger he had believed him and scared himself into thinking that the long shadows on the edge of the woods were forked tails winding off into lairs. When they reached the middle of the lake, they baited lines and dropped them over, drifting almost imperceptibly. "We'll try the shallows later," Brody said and then they were silent.

At first Lawson liked the faintly bitter smell of Brody's unlit cigar, which he still chewed on, and the lake, cool and unmoving as though it had not entirely wakened from the night. The first few bites made his heart pace faster. He held the pole tightly, trying to tense the muscles in his arms like the poised springs of a trap. But after the sun was well up and they had baited their hooks a number of times, Brody sighed, unshipped the oars, and began pulling slowly for the shore while Lawson trolled in the stern. They stopped again when Lawson had a good bite, and Brody tried too. But nothing came of it.

When the sun began to be hot enough so that Lawson did not need his jacket, his skin began to prickle, and the aluminum sides of the boat were getting hot to the touch, he lost interest. He rested the pole on the side of the boat, imagining the blank water under them, the fish off some other end of the lake, and his minnowed hook hanging plumb and useless. His father would have found the right spot immediately and, as usual, Brody was only second best. Above all he began to be irritated that his uncle did not seem to care whether they caught fish or not and that he enjoyed sitting in the boat, tonguing that wet end of his cigar.

"Well, anyway, it's a fine day," Brody said finally. "Just a few more minutes and we might try the bass. Have we got the bugs with us? Check that box there."

Lawson knew the bugs were there, and that his uncle probably knew also, but he checked anyway.

"Yep. There they are," Brody said when Lawson held them up. "You take that green-spotted one there. I had good luck with that one last year."

Lawson shrugged and put them down. He knew it would be best to answer politely, but he couldn't.

"What's the matter, old man? Cat got your tongue?"

Brody had put his pole down again and was easing out the oars. He paused with them out like wings, leaning on them.

"No."

"Discouraged?"

"Nope."

They were silent for a minute. Then Brody took the cigar out of his mouth, stared at it, and laid it gently on the thwart that lay between them.

"Sonny, I think maybe it's time we had a long talk. I know you don't care much for talking with me, but I can see there's something worrying you too. Let's have it out."

His uncle spoke quietly. Lawson looked at Brody, whose lips were slightly pursed, eyes not at all as foolish as they usually seemed.

"Your father should be talking to you now, but he seems too busy."

"I don't know why anyone should talk to me anyway. I haven't done anything wrong."

"Now I didn't say that, did I? You don't just talk to people when they've done wrong. Besides that's talking at them. I'm speaking about talking with you."

"I talk to Dad all the time."

But Lawson suspected that was one of those lies that trapped him.

"I don't know when. None of us see him much. Is that one of the things on your mind?"

"I suppose."

"You know, Lawson, that we're all concerned about your dad, don't you? I mean I don't want you to think you're alone in all this." Brody paused, looking down at his hands, and rubbed the oars slightly. Lawson could not remember his uncle seeming this embarrassed before. "We all love him very much, your mother and Esther and me."

Looking out now over the lake, frowning, his face was scarlet. Suddenly Lawson wanted to help him.

"I know."

"You do?" Brody leaned forward. "Then we can talk. I was a little afraid you wouldn't want to. Bailey and I, we always used to be so close, as brothers, and this summer, it's as though, as though . . ."

Lawson let him pause, watched the man's hand saw the air, briefly letting the oar-tip fall into the water and sink slowly.

"As though we've never been so close, or almost close, and yet so damned far away that I'm even afraid to talk to him, d'you understand?"

Lawson nodded.

"Here we are, in a home, a place that's as much your father's as mine. At least I think it's your father's too, and I've always told him so, and this summer he came and you and Jacqueline, and in the beginning I thought, what with the wedding and all, why this is going to be a grand time. There was your father with no need to go back right away, but then everything," and he reached down to take up the old cigar butt, and holding the oar with his elbow, he searched in his pocket for a match, "everything seemed to go wrong."

"Wrong?"

"Well, something, you know. You must feel it too."

Lawson never remembered talking about his father with anyone. He wasn't sure it was right.

"He seems OK."

Brody frowned. Lawson wanted to grasp the oars and pull to

shore. In any other place he could find a way out, but here, in the middle of the lake, there was none. His uncle was not going to give up.

"Lawson, I'm not trying to make you say something mean or anything like that. You see, Bailey won't really talk to any of us. Even your mother, and she's very worried. I thought that maybe, if there was anyone he had talked to it might be you and if so, something he said to you might help. I mean help us to understand, to help him."

When Brody had finished, he shipped the oars. He took out a handkerchief to wipe his brow. Lawson saw at last that his father was in some sort of trouble and that he, Lawson, was being asked to help.

"He hasn't. He hasn't talked to me about anything, Uncle Brody. What is all this about? Is my father sick?"

"No, no. I'm sorry, I didn't mean to alarm you. Sometimes people our age go through things that are very hard, and that's when they need friends who care for them. It's not all that serious."

But Lawson could tell Brody was lying, and that he thought it was serious. Brody looked at his wadded handkerchief, rolled it around, started to speak, stopped, and then burst out again.

"Look. He's never mentioned anything to you, has he?"

Lawson wanted only one thing: to get out of the boat. He didn't know anything about all this. But looking at his uncle's eyes moving nervously over his face, Lawson knew that even if he did, he wouldn't tell Brody or Esther or even his mother. And he wanted to find out on his own.

"You row me back, Uncle Brody. I'm no spy."

He gripped the side of the boat and everything began to blur, even the image of his uncle frowning, stammering slightly.

"Now, Lawson, damn it all, you took me all wrong."

"I want to get out. You take me back, take me back or I'll jump out."

He stood. The boat wobbled under him. He started to lose his balance, lurched back, and found himself sitting in the seat again.

"Hold on. Hold on. All right, we're headed back," and although Lawson could not see clearly anymore he felt the oars begin to bite, the steady tugging for shore, and all the way back Brody kept up a steady attempt at soothing. But Lawson did not listen. When they reached the shore he clambered over the side, up to his knees in the water, ran awkwardly toward the trees, feeling the hand try to grab him as he passed the white bulk of shirt and trousers that was his uncle saying, "It's just between us, sonny, between us," and then he was free to run along the path to the fields and the house. He did not want to see anyone. He found the hole under the house, squeezed through, and crouched there, his face against his upthrust knees. After a while he heard his uncle come in, heard him talking with Esther, and then Brody called him a few times from the porch. But he was not going to answer, not anyone, even his mother when she called too.

He stayed where he was until lunch. At the table he acted as though nothing had happened, and when his uncle started to say something to him, he stared at him so hard that the man stopped. Late that afternoon he was proud of the way he had acted. The main thing was he had stood up for his father, and he felt they had won a victory in some territory that was not clearly defined yet. But he would be ready when the next attack came.

They left him alone. He finished building the fort in the barn. There wasn't much to do in it by himself. He watched his father carefully now when he saw him. Brody was right. He did act strangely. There was almost no way to catch his attention, and for long periods of time he disappeared.

10

Bailey knew they were watching him now. The fact that no one except Jacqueline mentioned his retreat from the party showed how cautious they had become. Even her questions were tentative, and when he snapped back that he couldn't stand listening to another one of Brody's damned jokes, she did not press him. He began to find it convenient that they thought him disturbed, excusing his eccentricities, and he even took an odd pleasure in knowing they would never guess what was really going on.

He became impatient for his meetings with Nora. Once they did not see each other for three days, and when the afternoon they had agreed on arrived, Bailey reached the lake too early. As he walked up and down the shore he worried about the black thunder cloud that he could see rising slowly behind High Peak. If it began storming she might think he would not come. Maybe she did not even remember about today, or had made another date. She was a whorish little stoat, he could see that now. She had given in so easily to him, probably had been with lots of older men before, knew her way around the county. Over the lake a wet-smelling wind rumpled in toward him. What was he doing, wasting his time on her like this, why should he care whether she came or went? His insides twisted up and he imagined her naked, behind some shabby barroom, and rows of urine-reeking local red-necks were lining up to take her.

But then she called his name and he turned to see her standing near the edge of the woods. The lake darkened.

"Look," he said, "I know a place. An old fishing shack nearby. We'd be safer there anyway. I think we can make it."

They took the path up to the field and she ran across ahead of him, lithe and fast as a slim boy. She was laughing when he reached her.

"What's so funny?" he said, taking the braid from her hair with one hand, and she shook her head so that the locks whipped his cheek.

"I don't know. I don't know."

They went quickly down the trail to the river. She swung beside him, easy gaited, not out of breath at all.

"Have you ever been here?" he said when they reached the bend and the shack was in sight.

"Oh, sure."

They ran the last few yards because rain began to fall in pelting drops. They found the driest place where the roof was still whole. At first they stood holding hands and looking out to the slash of water, so heavy and hard now that he could not hear her when she said something. The thunder dropped and rolled, lightning sometimes flicked so brightly that it hurt his eyes. She leaned against him, her arm tight around his waist. But soon the worst was past, the rain came down in gusts, and all around them rose the wet, rotting smell of old leaves and earth. They made a bed with their clothes. He could not get enough of her. Again and again they whirled and tumbled against each other. He kneeled and touched her distant face, he bit and tasted and wanted to be her body. Finally he felt a great emptiness. The light that came through the shattered roof was colorless, and they lay side by side without moving.

"I fed the pigs this morning," he said slowly. "Do you like pigs?"

She tittered. "Pigs? Whatever are you talking about, Bailey?"

"No, I mean it. Pigs. Have you ever watched them much?"

"Lord, no. I can't bear them. I mean it's not the smell and all, which God knows is bad enough. They just have the ugliest faces."

But he kept looking at the white holes above him.

"Well, I watched them today. I mean really watched them. There's nothing wrong with them. They have their own lives. We make them pretty much the way they are. If they weren't all penned up, if they just wandered around they'd not be so bad. At least they wouldn't have to wallow in their own shit."

"They're ugly, that's all," and she put her face against his shoulder.

"I thought of the pigs in the Bible. The madmen tending the pigs? and how they could say nothing but 'raca, raca,' and Christ came and cast their demons into the pigs and the pigs went crazy and plunged over a cliff, drowned in the ocean. So much for the evil spirits."

She wasn't listening, and he could not remember why he had started talking about the pigs anyway. They would have to get dressed and go home. "Raca, raca," he murmured, and wondered if it really meant something.

She seemed reluctant to let go of him when they parted, and that too depressed him, the gentle, clinging motion of her hand as she released his.

But the two days until their next meeting dragged. Food was dull, celluloid and pasty to his mouth. The sun was mere weight on his skin, and when people spoke to him, he was more aware of their mouths moving than of the actual sounds they made. He knew he should be frightened, but somehow even that emotion evaded him. His energy was poured into the idea of their meetings, and all other time was drained and blotted up. He tried walking to all the places he liked. There was only a flat field, or a stump, or a tree like any other tree leaning over a very ordinary fence. Nothing struck out or jagged him. He walked to the barn in the evening to watch the cows yoked to their stalls, chewing vacantly, blowing through their wet, wide nostrils. Leaning there, he was startled to hear his own voice say to them, "What have I done?" He jerked his hand purposely down the roughhewn beam he leaned against, pitting his flesh against the grain. Anything to feel again. The pain pricked slightly as if his hand had gone to sleep, and yet when he looked, the palm was embedded with slivers, and one finger was gashed and bleeding. He took out the splinters deliberately, and although it began to ache numbly, his own hand was a fish, foreign to him. Working the pump handle, he soaked it in the sudden flow of cold water and then went down to the lake to watch the sun set.

That night he woke with a start. Jacqueline was turning and moaning in the dark beside him. A breeze puffed in, dragging one curtain against the chair. Suddenly the other person who moved in the room was very specific—Jacqueline Ambler, that woman he had loved and lived with for years now, a fact, a separate person, and her moaning made him think of her as something wounded or violated, as though they were both locked tightly into a huge closet and he could barely see her, rumpled down near him like a bulky piece of clothing that had slipped off its hanger, the other hangers swaying and jangling as though the fall had just taken place. He wanted to find the door, to run out because a killer was in the room. "Jacqueline?" he whispered, but she did not wake, and his own voice cut through the dark to return him to their own room, the familiar window turning gray now. There was no killer. Except himself. He lay back, throwing the covers off, sweating profusely. There it was. His wife, his son, his own life—what was he doing? It was a moral question, after all, wasn't it? They would leave the next day. He would even get up now, before dawn, and begin packing. What had come over him? For a few minutes he was more terrified than he had ever been in his life.

But just as quickly he lay in an absolute calm. He felt his ribs and how he had lost enough weight in the past weeks so that the flesh on his belly no longer gathered in folds when he lay slightly curved, the way he had looked when he was younger. He ran his hand across his thighs and then cupped his testicles in his palm, and the shaft of his penis stirred slightly to his touch as though its own life, to which he was connected by a frail net, went on without him. Then he dozed.

That afternoon they met at the shed and once again they began eagerly, without words, touching each other as though trying to read Braille. But later she wanted to talk.

"Wait a while," she said, as if he were being greedy. She talked aimlessly, said something about how one of her friends had become pregnant and had to go to that awful place in Roanoke where they kept unwed mothers and how if it ever happened to her she would find a way of killing it before it got a good start. She'd taken more hot baths in the past few days than anyone ever had, she suspected, and hoped her aunt wasn't catching on because she had said something about how Nora must be the cleanest girl in town. She kept up an endless chatter, full of strange small-town notions, and Bailey held silent as long as he could, the words, the tone of her voice beginning to surround and drag him down.

"Well, you won't be pregnant," he said abruptly.

"How do you know?"

She turned slightly, flicking the ash of her cigarette, and then touched one breast with her hand. "I'm sore all over. How can you be so sure? We've done it enough and besides it doesn't take much."

"You won't be. You're just being melodramatic."

"But what if I was? What would you do?"

"Me?"

"I mean, you'd be the father. There'd be no mistaking that. And you're married. I guess I'd be left holding it all, wouldn't I? You'd just go away. Had your fun, gone home."

He did not like her bitterness. Overacted, it reminded him again of how young she was. She crushed out the cigarette.

"Well, I don't care. Maybe I'd have the baby. Maybe I'll go ahead and have it and always remember that it's yours."

What was she doing? Surely she knew how idiotic it was.

"Bailey, I think I love you."

"Love me?"

He leaned up abruptly on his elbows and stared at her. Her eyes were opened wide.

"Yes. I do. I know I do. What's so odd about that?"

He laughed once, bitterly.

"You don't love me. Lord, child, love isn't something that just, that just . . ." But he stopped because she was obviously going to cry and he could not go on anyway. Too tired. Hell, what was love, anyway? What did he know about it? She had as much right to say that as he had to deny it.

"I'm sorry, Nora. I'm sure you do."

"I do, I do. I did almost right from the start. You were so good to me, and we talked so easy and all, and I knew we were meant for each other. I mean, do you think I could do all these things with any man? Do you?"

She twisted her wet face up for a moment and then placed it back against him, calming slightly.

"Oh, I've done it before, I know, but I could never make love with a man I didn't love, that would be whoring, just plain whoring."

He looked down the tanned curve of neck, the white strips where her halter had been, to the dark fold of her buttocks and legs drawn up against him. She turned her face slightly, looking up at the roof now, her eyes a little puffed. Lord, he was bored. What game did they have to act out next?

"You're just playing with me, aren't you?" She sat up, her

hair wisped over her face. "You're going to play with me for a while and then when you're through and the summer's over you're going to leave me and go away."

"Child, what do you expect?"

"Don't call me a child. I'm not a child, you hear, I'm not."

She stood up now, looking down at him, fists clenched. Looking at her body, which was like a shaft of molded light, he realized that he did not care for her at all as a person. Only her body interested him, and he looked at it, feeling his own flesh begin to rise at the sight of it.

He kneeled and slowly molded with his hands up her body as though he were turning white clay on a whirling wheel.

"Don't. I mean it, Bailey. I won't ever again," but she already had her hands on his neck.

She calmed down before they parted.

"I'm so silly," she said, but Bailey worried as he watched her precede him through the woods. He felt almost nothing at the thought of her going or at the idea of their meeting again. What would there be left if even this fell blank? But he would see, he would see when the time came.

Two, maybe three meetings later, he knew there was no further to go. Events around him were more and more jumbled, and only a few stuck in his mind, like the argument with Brody when he wanted to take Lawson fishing and for some reason Bailey found himself saying no, an answer that neither of them expected and that Brody took as an insult. Bailey relented, or he thought he did, telling them that they could certainly both go fishing and that he had only been joking—or did he? He found it increasingly difficult to distinguish between the things that really happened and those he imagined. A day or two after that he met her again in the shed. This time she was there before he came. She seemed remote.

"I'm tired."

Looking at her face in the shaft of light, he decided she did look haggard, dark circles under her eyes. He took off his clothes, turned to watch her do the same, noticing how mechanically they stripped now, piling the articles neatly in one place, unrolling the blanket they kept there. And when she was naked, facing him, Bailey saw nothing but skin and hair and dabs of color like a hood of flesh, always concealing. He felt nothing. Absolutely nothing. She was a haunch of beef hung in cold storage. Who was she, anyway? This Nora, body, tongue and words and breathing. He walked over to her. She was looking at him in a puzzled way, so he knew his thoughts showed on his face. He stood close to her, not touching, and looked at her body slowly, as if trying to find something recognizable, something to snag him. But his mind was blank and smooth. Her breasts, pointed up, were hung on her chest like two lumps of soft muscle. Her lips were pink skin turned out. He put his hand down, her legs spread slightly and he touched the cleft, already moist. But it was nothing to him; wet folds as neutral as a dog's nose.

"What is it?" she said.

Suddenly he was angry, almost panicked. He took her by the shoulders and kissed her hard on the mouth.

"That hurts."

But he would not stop. He pulled her down on the blanket, spread her under him, kissed her again, pressing against her mouth so hard that his teeth hurt. She was breathing heavily, wide-eyed. He thrust at her with his hips, as though he would mash her into the soil. But nothing happened. She stopped struggling, closed her eyes, and took the tongue he thrust at her.

He jerked away from her and lay on his back.

"What's wrong."

"I can't."

She leaned over him. His body was numbing all over. He fought for a moment to scramble back to it, but he was twisting, falling away, getting colder.

"Please," she whined, "please."

He looked at her, her face flushed, one lip even slightly seamed with red where he had pressed her, and he began laughing, quietly at first, but as he saw her face grow more puzzled, he could not control himself, and laughed harder and harder.

"What's the matter with you?"

She pulled away from him, reached suddenly for her clothes, and held them against her as though she were naked to a stranger. Then she began to dress, carefully, keeping her eyes on him all the time.

"Are you going?" and he put his hands behind his head.

"I sure am. I don't know what's come over you, but I think you're cracked."

"Maybe."

"I've had enough of you anyway," and she began to wind her skirt around her hips. She stood, smoothing her blouse down.

"Enough?"

"You don't care about me at all. You don't care about anything. You're just making fun of me."

She was more frightened than her words indicated, but she was suddenly proud, tossing her hair back with a shrug and bunching it behind her head with her hands.

"I suppose I am."

"Besides, you don't love me. I know you don't. And I don't need you. You're only one man, you know."

So she was tired of him now, had probably found someone else, more her age. He imagined her crying to some drawling mountain boy, raising his adolescent indignation with her story.

She went to the door, stood there for a moment half-turned, hesitant. He was surprised to see that she was crying, her face uncontorted but wet.

"Nora," he said hollowly. "Nora Smith."

"Oh, you. You. You even say my name like you'd never heard

it before. You're horrible," and she wheeled, slipping out the door and leaving the view of a hemlock trunk and some bushes dashed with sunlight.

So that was it. He felt no sense of loss. After a few moments he became aware that he felt very little of anything. The bole of a tree, some bushes tangled around it, a tilted doorway, late afternoon light. He was naked. He rolled over on his back, hands under his head. When he closed his eyes he could not even see or remember her face and did not know how long he lay there. Maybe an hour or two. For a long time he concentrated on the image of the backyard in Richmond. No one there, not even himself. Only the yard with its circular path and the defunct fountain and the gum tree spread out near the wall. He tried to guess the season by looking at the tree. But when he stared hard it seemed to shift into the corner of his eyes, and he could not tell whether there were leaves or not. He had to know. He turned uncomfortably on the ground as though the image in his head were fixed and by moving he could gain a different perspective. The tree would not focus, and he began to hear a voice that hardly paused for breath, seemed to carry on an undertoned narration. He tried to make out the words. It reminded him of the constant chatter he had kept up as a child when he played by himself in the sand and gravel. But this was his older voice. Who was he talking to?

Bailey sat up with a jerk. Dusk. He climbed hastily into his clothes, not bothering to tie his shoes, and began running back through the woods.

At first he was not sure where he was going or why he was in such a hurry. He scrambled across the field toward the barn, running as if pursued in a dream. Inside he went directly to the peg where Brody kept the revolver hanging. His "crow stabber," he called it. It was loaded. He let himself catch his breath and then went out past the lumped haystacks to the corncrib. He leaned on one hand for a moment, fingering the dry ridges of a cob. All his edges and boundaries were fading into the landscape. What was he? Certainly not a husband. Not much of a father, even. But none of these things mattered. A father, that was only someone who blew a pod of seeds into a womb. Lawson. The boy was him, part of him—carrying his cells. He was there, in those cells, mindless. Probably the best way to be—in the cells, unconscious.

He looked once at the barely discernible line where land and sky met. Lord, Lord, all he wanted was a kind of resurrection, but there was no way to burst through. He swung the pistol hastily in an arc to his head. Wait, he said, but what he heard was a great blast that opened out a field, all gray and stubbled, from which a flock of blackbirds rose startled into a steel sky and dispersed like chips of metal sinking away.

11

That afternoon Lawson was high in the loft looking for pigeons' nests and the mottled eggs they sometimes held. He liked to pick them up and cup them in the palm of his hand. They were warm and smooth and the pigeons fluttered nearby until he put the eggs back and moved away. From the hatchway he could see down across the fields where the cows were splotches of black and white, hardly moving. Footsteps thudded slowly under him, and then his father's head appeared. He was going to call to him, but crouched back against the wall. Bailey did not look up, but to both sides, and then started down the cattle path and climbed the fence. When he reached the gully Lawson jumped onto the haystack below and began to follow him. Lying on his stomach at the top of the ridge, he saw him enter the woods. He ran after him, heart pounding.

Maybe to be with him, he thought at first, but as soon as he entered the woods, saw the brown flick of his father's shirt among the trees, he changed his mind. He wanted to know where he was going. He wanted to know more than Brody and all of them.

When the figure disappeared, Lawson ran, and sometimes when he almost caught up to him he had to duck behind a tree, holding his breath for fear he could be heard. His father was walking fast, but never seemed to look back. Lawson was scared and did not know why. He kept turning as though the trees themselves were following him, and once when a chipmunk scurried and chittered away in the leaves he jumped aside. When they reached the clearing and bend in the river, his father paused, crossed to the shack, and stooped inside.

Lawson worked his way around the edge of the clearing where he stood and listened carefully. He was certain he heard voices. Suddenly a girl walked across the doorway. He stared at the cabin, but she did not appear again, and he moved forward as far as he could under the cover of the trees. Still he was more than fifty feet away. There was no sound now.

He crouched low and ran to the corner, stood very still against the log post, trying to keep his breathing silent. He heard nothing. Turning slightly to one of the windows on his left he brought his face level with it then gradually let his head move over the threshold until he could see in with one eye.

At first everything was too dim, then he began to see the bright cracks where light shone through the walls and roof. A man was standing on the bare floor with his back to Lawson. He was naked, and so was the girl who faced him. She was Nora. They weren't moving, but seemed to stare at each other. She reached up and touched one breast as if offering it to him. The man turned his head slightly.

His father. Lawson could not move. If there had been nothing to lean against he would have fallen in. Words came tumbling to him, jammed against his throat. He could not breathe. His father naked, and Nora stepping forward to move her hand slowly up and across his bare chest. Bailey's eyes moved, seemed to pause directly at the point where Lawson's face was, but without expression. Lawson ducked, waiting for the sound of his father's voice. Nothing.

He began running through the woods, bumping into trees, stumbling until he reached the river and the island beyond it. Without pausing he waded through the waist-deep water, plunged and swam, wanting only to get far enough into the brush and pines to be out of sight. There, breathless and almost sick with running, he sat against the bole of a tree. Lawson closed his eyes. Once again his father's face was turned toward him, the mouth open now, forming words but without sound, and her hand stroked up and down the chest.

Everything was the same when he opened them. The river was tumbling off beyond the trees. Lawson stood up too quickly so that he had to lean with one hand against the tree for a minute. He had no idea what to do. He couldn't go home. His father would know as soon as he looked at him. For a while he wandered around on the island as if it were a cage, shivering in his wet clothes. There was only one thing to do. He had to run away. He sat again for a long time and stared so hard at the river that when he looked up the banks seemed to move. Finally rolling his pants up more tightly, he found a place to wade across upstream and walked back toward the cabin in the evening light.

This time he did not sneak up to the window. He came to the cabin from the river side, across the beach, and circled around to pause in front of the door. There was no sound.

No one was there. The cabin was just as he had remembered it, except the dirt floor was scuffed and marked. He kneeled where he had seen his father. The dirt was hard-packed. There was no way to tell how recently anyone had been there. All around him in the semidark he could see the white droppings of cigarette butts. He picked up one and turned it around. The tip was red with lipstick and he threw it away as though it might still burn him. On the way to the door he saw a bundle of cloth in one corner but he did not go nearer. There was barely enough light for him to get back to the island. He was not hungry. He would start out tomorrow. The sun went down and he curled up, waiting for sleep to come.

Why had he followed his father? He wanted all this to be a dream, wanted to go back to the barn and stand there and watch his father leave. Maybe he could forget it all. But he knew he never would, and he imagined cutting into that part of him that knew and throwing it away. In the dark he wondered what they would be doing at home, if they would have called the police to find him. His mother would be very upset. But how could he ever look at any of them again without showing what he knew? If they had even come to see how he felt about Bonnie, this was much too big to hide.

Everything began to disconnect. He was asleep. No, he was awake, and the alarm had rung and it was time for school. His mother was impatient, knocking on his bedroom door. "The bus will be here any moment. Now hurry." No, that couldn't be. He could see the barn from the window, so it had to be summer. No school. "Look, mother," he yelled, "you've forgotten where we are." But no one answered. Downstairs the living room had been burned and scorched. His yellow slicker had melted and smelled of burned rubber. "Who's been sitting in my chair?" a large voice kept repeating. The river rose suddenly and swept the porch away and Lawson tried to get into the attic where the canoe was stored, but everyone was sleeping there with the door locked, and they couldn't hear him knocking.

When the trees began to take dim shapes out of the night, he was certain he had not slept. All he remembered was being very tired, and no matter where he turned or how he placed himself his body was on a slant. At one time the ground was shifting him toward the river. The sound of water grew louder and louder. But later it dimmed and the night itself came down like a fog, making it difficult to breathe. He was very frightened once and called out, but his voice, so loud and hollow, did not sound like his own, and he was silenced. He began to think that what he had seen meant he would have to do something more than run away, but he did not know what. Would he have to tell his mother? That did not seem right. Talk to his father? But the distance between himself and his father seemed total. Why, he said, why, as the birds began to chirp and warble in the dawn, did he have to follow him? He wanted to die. If only he could die. He stopped thinking, rolled back into sleep.

He shivered and sat up, half-dreaming, in the chill before the sun came up fully. Awake now. The dream faded. No, he did not want to die at all, and he had seen very clearly what that was—just himself, but not himself any longer, in a black much darker than any night, and with no eyes anymore even to see the black coming through him like a wind, blowing him back, away from himself, reeling like a leaf.

He had to see his father. He picked up his shoes and socks and crossed the river. On the other side he paused long enough to put them on without bothering to tie the laces. By the time he reached the house they were all unbound and flapping loosely.

He pushed the screen door. The sun was hardly up, and yet he could see everyone standing around in the living room, fully dressed. His mother was crying and leaning against Esther who was staring out past her at Brody. And Brody, his hair all tousled and on end, had his head bowed, hands plunged in his pockets, and shirt cuffs undone.

"I know it was just an accident," his mother sobbed, and Esther said something that Lawson could not hear.

The only one who was not there was his father.

"Dad?" and he stepped into the hall.

Brody turned, his face puffy and shocked.

"Thank heavens, here's the child now," and he began to move forward.

But Lawson did not care about them. He only wanted to see his father.

"Dad?" but by this time Brody had reached him and he let himself be guided toward his mother and Esther.

"Where have you been?" Jacqueline wailed, clasping him so that he could see over her shoulder to Esther.

"Your father," Esther said, "has shot himself."

12

For a few days Lawson was shuffled about from room to room, told to play outside and leave the grown-ups alone, told by his mother to stay close to her, told by Esther not to bother his mother at a time like this, commiserated with by Brody, until finally he broke, went in tears to the kitchen and sat where he knew little would be said and nothing asked of him. And he was right. Emily went about her business, glancing at him from time to time, and when James came in they talked quietly together and did not bother him.

After his father was brought back from the hospital, the doctor came and went twice a day. They discussed whether Bailey should have stayed longer, but the doctor assured them it was only a flesh wound with a bad concussion, and that all he needed was peace and quiet. Lawson was allowed to go upstairs once to see him. He was asleep, as he was most of the time now because of the drugs, his head bound in white bandages, a shock of black hair like crow feathers sticking up and over them as though he were dressed for a ceremonial dance, and his face so blank and tired that Lawson was afraid they had lied to him and that his father was really dying. His mother seemed to have been crying for days even though they kept telling him his father would live. He would have to stay in bed for a long time. But they stayed shocked, overtalkative, or apt to sit in complete silence through a meal.

They would not let him talk to his father, even for a moment. He needed to. He would lie restlessly in his bed at night, thinking of what he would say or ask. All he needed were a few words. Why was he there with Nora, and what was he, Lawson, supposed to do now? Everything in his own life was hanging in space, waiting for his father to speak, move, do something. The house, the landscape, all the people held still like the figure of his father wrapped and mute on white sheets.

He had to break it somehow. The guardian figures of his aunt and uncle and mother were in a constant vigil at the bedside or hovering in the hall, and his father was still in too much pain to talk anyway. At first he thought of going to Bonnie. But he heard Esther talking about how she and Charlie had gone on a trip together and whether they should call and tell her. Jacqueline said no, don't spoil it for them, and Brody agreed. Finally he knew whom he should talk to, even if it made him angry to think of her, so one morning he walked out the driveway and down the road toward town.

It was hot and had not rained for a week. Each time a trailer truck passed he felt mashed, and the grit they threw up rasped between his teeth. He knew she lived in the white house behind the drugstore.

Her aunt came to the door. Lawson tried to look as though he knew what he were doing.

"Yes?"

"Nora. Is Nora in?"

The woman looked vacantly at him and then half-closed one eye.

"Aren't you Bailey Wright's boy?"

"Yes, ma'm."

"Well, come on in," and she had a hand on his shoulder before he could step back. "Nora?" she cried as she shut the door, but Nora was already there, a pale face and legs and arms in the doorway to the living room.

"I'm right here."

"Here's Bailey's boy. He's asking for you."

"I know," she said quietly. "I heard."

Lawson stood awkwardly in the hallway between the two women, suddenly realizing he had no idea of what to do next.

"I heard about your father, sonny," and the old lady paused as if out of breath. "I think it's just awful. I guess no matter how long you've been handling guns they're never safe, are they?"

Lawson did not answer. He was staring at Nora's face, and as his eyes adjusted to the dim, stuffy interior of the house, he could see she did not know what to do either.

"Come on in, Lawson," and he went where she seemed to be directing him, toward the sofa against the far wall of the cluttered little room.

For a moment her aunt stood in the doorway as if undecided what to do.

"It's all right. I think he wants to talk to me, don't you, Lawson?"

"Yes," and Lawson looked at the aunt almost angrily, as if his eyes could push her away. She turned and walked off limping, one foot seeming heavier than the other.

Nora sat beside him. He turned and stared at her face, her eyes that blinked at him like an animal who knows it is being watched.

"Did he send you?" she whispered.

At first he did not understand the question. Who? Send what? Then he was angry.

"No. I came on my own."

Her eyes kept moving over his face.

"I know," he blurted. "I know about you. I saw you in the cabin. Naked."

He watched the eyes narrow, the mouth turn hard.

"How? Were you spying?"

"I followed him. I went through the woods and saw him go in the cabin and then I saw you there too."

"So?"

But suddenly he wasn't angry. He was losing the questions he wanted to ask.

"He tried to kill himself," and he felt his voice wobbling. "Dad tried to. He did, I know it. Why?"

She had raised a hand to her throat quickly and then put it back in her lap. "It's very hard to explain. It's about love. It's very romantic and you're too young to understand. Sometimes people do that when they're in love and unhappy."

"Why? What's wrong with him? I don't understand."

He began to lose sight of her.

"We went there all the time, Lawson. We loved each other. But I left him and it's all over now."

"No. You did something to him. What did you do? What happened to him?"

She was standing. "No, I didn't. I didn't at all. He was crazy. Your father's crazy, that's all."

"He is not. He's not," and he had to stop for fear he would begin crying. "You did something."

"Yes, he is too. He just started doing crazy things. I didn't do anything to him, Lawson," and then there was a bitterness in her voice that made him draw back from any grief, as if she were shaking him hard. "Oh, he probably sent you here, didn't he? Him or your Uncle Brody, or Esther. To pick on me. They all know, don't they? They all want to say it's my fault 'cause they can't face the fact a Wright might be a crazy, dirty old man. They never did like me being with Bonnie. Never did think I was the right kind of friend for her. You Wrights. You all think you're so big up there on your hill. Well, you're not, that's all. You're not," and suddenly she was the one who was crying, and he could not speak as she hunched back onto the sofa.

"Nobody sent me." He only wanted to go now. It was getting worse, not clearer.

She looked at him and stopped crying, and after a while she got up and blew her nose and then sat down again.

"I'm sorry. I don't understand."

The words went around in his head.

"Why?" he blurted. "I want to know. If you don't understand, who does?"

Uneven footfalls were coming down the stairs, the aunt passed again in the hallway, her face staring in unconcealed curiosity. Nora sat there, her face puffed, mouth slightly open. He stood and then began backing toward the door. She held up one hand.

"Wait. Lawson, don't go yet."

She started to walk toward him with her hand out. He backed wildly into a small table, heard it topple and something that had been on top of it smashed. "Nora?" the voice came from down the hall, and he turned, bolted through the screen door, and ran without looking back.

When he reached home Lawson locked himself in his room. His mother pleaded with him. Brody tried to use a knife on the lock, but it broke off. He did not want to see anyone. He did not even want to see. He pulled the curtains and lay face down on his covers. He had seen too much and all of it was totally confused in his mind. By noon he was not even answering when they called. He knew his mother was becoming frantic, but he did not care. He put out both of his arms and clutched at the sides of the mattress as though if he did not hold on, the bed would tip and roll him out. "Lawson, please, Lawson," his mother called. Finally Uncle Brody came red-faced and straining up a ladder and in the window. "Damned foolishness," and he wrenched the lock open to let the women in as Lawson turned his head to stare at him. "I'm too old to go clambering ladders like that. I'd give the boy a good whipping, I would," but the women were not about to do that and his mother kept brushing at the hair on his forehead.

"It's all been too much," Esther said.

For a while his mother sat alone with him and then persuaded him to come down to the living room where it was cooler. The shades were all pulled against the heat, and Esther had made some lemonade. Brody was sitting on the couch, his shirt open, and he shook the glass from time to time to make the ice rattle.

"At least it sounds cool," he said.

But Lawson did not want to sit there and talk about nothing, and he did not know how they could do it. Esther gave him a glass of lemonade and he sat down in the chair by the desk. He watched them move and drink and settle into a tense silence. His father was upstairs lying in bed. Somehow Lawson began to feel they were all dead, that the house was covered over with turf and that they were all waiting for air to run out.

"Why did Dad try to shoot himself?" he said loudly and watched them jerk their heads to him as though he had himself fired a pistol.

"Your father did not, Lawson," and his mother's firm tone of voice seemed less directed at him than at the other two. "It was an accident."

"I'm sorry, Jacqueline," Brody said. "I don't think it right to not face the facts. Now Bailey won't speak to us yet, I know, and until then there's . . ."

Jacqueline interrupted. "There's no telling. So why talk about it or bring it up again?"

Brody raised both of his hands. "I didn't. I've argued enough with you about this. But I still say it's best to look at things as they are. It's going to make things easier later, that's all."

Esther put a hand on Jacqueline's knee and spoke gently.

"He's right, you know. We've got to face the fact that Bailey needs some help, probably, and I don't mean Doctor Johns's, either."

But Jacqueline sat very stiffly as though her knees had turned into marble.

"You're all so set against him. But I know Bailey. Even if he's been tired and upset he'd never do a thing like that."

Brody leaned forward, emphasizing his point with a finger. They seemed to have forgotten about Lawson who watched tensely, wondering at what he had set going. "Exactly the thing. Just what I remember folks saying after Uncle Eustace died. I tell you, you never think it possible. It's such an incomprehensible thing that when it happens it's got to seem an accident."

"Oh, here you are his own brother and you say a thing like that."

"Well, don't you understand, Jacqueline? It's because I am his brother and I love him that I say we've got to begin with the facts or we'll never get to the bottom of it all, and we've got to do that if we're to be any help."

She suddenly seemed to relax, sitting back in her chair, the glass of lemonade from which she was not drinking cupped in her hands.

"I know, Brody. I didn't mean to sound as though I don't believe you love him. It's just so hard."

Esther cooed, "We're overwrought, we're all overwrought," and she looked grimly at her husband as if to silence him, but he could not be stopped now. As he spoke he ticked off points on his fingers.

"First off, there's no one here wouldn't say Bailey hasn't been himself of late. There's reason enough for that and more. Insecurity is one of your biggest worries for a man, and you've said yourself losing the job was getting to him. Then there's the fact, and I mean fact because I'm his own brother and we've been around guns since we were awful small, that Bailey couldn't make that kind of mistake with a hand gun. Now it might of gone off if it'd fallen on the floor or something, or if he was cleaning it, but you know when I came out and found him, the gun was lying right in his hand and he was gripping it like you'd fire it." Brody sat back, crossed his legs. "Jacqueline, honey, I hate to say it worse than poison, but we've got to start with the fact he tried to . . ."

"Brody Wright, you have no feelings at all," Esther shrilled. "Don't you see that boy sitting there like he's gonna bust?"

Brody cowered slightly, and looked guiltily at his nephew.

"Why?" and Lawson suddenly felt very cold with a mean, angry desire to watch them all talk some more. Even his mother. He mistrusted the way she defended his father, was jealous because he would never defend him again.

"Why what, Lawson?" Brody answered.

"Why did he try to kill himself?"

Again they were quiet for a moment.

"Lawson," Esther said slowly, "I don't know if anyone could explain that to you really. Sometimes a man gets so tangled up in himself that nothing seems right. Now it's wrong of a mortal to feel that way, but when he does, he doesn't see a way of getting out of all the things that are tying him round. So he tries to get as far away from it all as he can."

Jacqueline smiled weakly at her son and then looked at Esther as though she were very grateful for the way she put it.

"Tied up in what?" Lawson insisted.

"Oh, different things," Esther continued. "Now with Uncle Eustace they used to say . . ."

"I don't care about Uncle Eustace. What was my dad tied up in?"

Esther raised her eyebrows. "Well, I expect none of us really knows, Lawson."

"Your daddy was worried about his work," Brody said.

"It didn't bother him much when we were in Richmond. I heard him tell Mother that."

Lawson took a deep gulp of his lemonade and almost choked on it. He did not really want it, but for a moment he needed to put something between himself and the others.

Brody said, "Well. Is that so, Jacqueline?"

"Can't we talk about something else?"

For a moment they were silent. Brody shifted a little in his chair, picked up his glass, and tipped it to get one of the ice cubes into his mouth. He chewed and cracked at it.

"Jacqueline, Bailey never got into trouble before with anyone?" and then he stopped cold. Esther had raised a finger at him. "Esther, you just agreed we got to face the facts."

"Trouble?" Jacqueline said coldly. "No, it's all right, Esther. Let's get this out and done with now. Go on."

"Well, I think of our father. He had a certain weakness he was prone to. I've been watching Bailey lately and . . ."

"Brody Wright . . ."

"No, Esther. Let him speak out here and now. I don't want just some sort of vile insinuations. So help me, let's scotch this snake here and now. But you're going to have to say it, Brody Wright. In front of his own wife and child."

Brody wiped nervously at the back of his neck with one hand. "A man's got a right to a frailty here and there."

"Well. What is it?" Jacqueline said like a brittle schoolmistress.

"It seems to me . . ." Brody paused, took out his handkerchief, balled it up, and stared at his knees for a moment, then blurted ". . . that he's been spending an awful lot of time with Nora Smith lately."

"That's the limit, Brody." Esther stood.

But Jacqueline put up her hand. "Nonsense. It's the last I'm going to hear of that. Not once in his life has Bailey been unfaithful to me."

"Oh, Jacqueline, I'm so ashamed I could cry," Esther moaned. "Brody, you better ask forgiveness. It's just like a man to call such a thing a 'little frailty.' Haven't you ever heard of adultery?"

Brody kneaded his hands. He stammered, stopped, then said quietly, "I only remember my own father, and how he was the finest man ever, but there are some things a man can't control. And afterward he's probably pretty shamed."

"How would you know, Brody?" Esther said sharply.

"You may talk about your father all you want," and Jacqueline was less calm now, "but not my husband. He wouldn't do that."

"He did," and Lawson stood, his arms very stiff and fists balled against his hips. "He did, and I saw him."

His mother jumped up, one hand toward him as though she were trying to catch something he had thrown but she had missed and it struck her in the stomach. She sucked in her breath.

"What are you saying? Lawson, what are you saying?"

"It *was* Nora. They were down at the river in the shack. She and Dad were naked inside. I saw them."

His mother struck him once, very hard across the face, and would have again except that Esther held her arm. Then Lawson lost control. He had no one in mind, perhaps he would have even hit his mother if she was there, but Brody came by chance between them, and it took him a while to get behind Lawson and hold on where his flailing arms and feet could not hit him. But then Jacqueline was weeping, had her arms around him, was simultaneously trying to push Brody away and was saying, "Don't you hurt my boy, don't you hurt my boy," while Brody looked hopelessly over them to his wife and kept saying, "I was only trying to help."

Lawson stopped struggling and clung to his mother, not crying or speaking, and they both found their way to the couch. It was easy then to tell her what he had seen. She became very still. When he was through she put a hand under his chin and lifted his head.

"Lawson, this is very important. You wouldn't lie to me, would you?"

"No," but he wished he had. He felt he had done a terrible thing to his father. Jacqueline broke the silence and walked into the middle of the room.

"I've got to see Bailey."

Esther reached her and put a hand on her shoulder.

"Hold on, not now. We've all got to cool down. You know the doctor said he shouldn't be troubled. This is no time to . . ."

"I've got to see Bailey," and she brushed Esther's hand off her shoulder angrily. "Bailey," she called, but then she folded onto the chair. "No, I don't want to see him at all."

"Let's all sit down again," Esther said.

Brody put a hand on Lawson's back. "Maybe Lawson better leave the room."

"No," and Jacqueline looked up, putting out her hand. "I want my boy here."

He took her hand and sat on the arm of the chair, her fingers held tightly in his.

Esther said, "He's seen it all anyway. Lord knows what he thinks of grown-ups now."

"It's all right," and his mother was staring at him. "My boy is strong. You don't hate us for all this, do you, Lawson?"

He shook his head.

Brody said, "Look here. Now we don't know . . ."

"We know enough. Or at least I do."

"Let's try to keep some perspective," Esther began.

"I have. Enough to make me sick. I guess I've always wondered if he could. But I never thought he really would. Not Bailey."

"We don't know anything for sure," and Brody put his back to the mantelpiece. "Not till we hear from Bailey."

But Jacqueline did not seem to hear him. She was staring hard at the hands in her lap. For a moment no one spoke, and Lawson could heard his own heart pounding in his ears. When she looked up again, his mother's face was very severe but she was staring hard at the window. "Lawson and I are going home today, Esther. We'll pack up and start this afternoon."

"Now, Jacqueline."

"No. I mean it."

"But," and Esther looked at Brody and then at her, "what about Bailey? He's hurt, he needs you."

"Needs me?" She gripped Lawson's hand. "He'll be all right. I don't want to see him for a while."

Esther shook her head. "This is just what you can't allow. This is a marriage that you're walking out on."

Jacqueline actually laughed. "I am?" Then she became serious. "I didn't say I'm leaving forever, Esther. I don't want to see him or this place for a while. Especially this place. I need some time to think," and she squeezed Lawson's arm so hard that he almost drew back.

"But now's the time to be among friends. I know we aren't much help . . ."

"No, right now you're not."

That seemed to stiffen Esther a little. Her voice was almost pettish.

"It's not right. We don't know anything yet about how Bailey feels. Why, he's probably so ashamed he tried to kill himself. When he comes around, you've got to be here."

"Ashamed," Jacqueline murmured.

"Yes. Why not? And besides, you remember the words, don't you? 'In sickness and in health'? The real test of a marriage comes when . . ."

"Oh, stop," and Jacqueline stood. "God, I'm so tired of all this. Just let us go."

Lawson could not understand it. Esther seemed to get more and more desperate.

"You can't walk away like this. You're running away from it."

"All right, then. All right," and Jacqueline turned, two red spots burning in her cheeks, which Lawson knew happened only when she was unbearably angry. "I'm running away. I'm sick of this place. I'm sick of the Wrights and their damned inbred little backwoods' history. What has it all meant to me but Uncle Eustace who killed himself and father Thomas who drank and whored around the country and now they're both upstairs perched on my husband's shoulder. I want out. I want out, you hear?"

Brody lowered his head, lips pursed.

"Now, hold on. We know we can't match any Amblers for their fine history, but there's no family doesn't have its troubles and I won't have you laying into ours and blaming everything on us. After all, my brother's been a support to his family and worked hard, and it's other people's families who have brothers like Edward who go in and out of loony bins all their lives and live off old ladies and . . ."

But Jacqueline did not give him time to finish. Lawson felt a tug, and his mother walked firmly out of the room with him in tow. There were some apologies before they left, but it was all very stiff. "I'll call every day," his mother said. He knew she did not drive well, but he was not worried. In the car he tried to say something to her, but all she did was put a hand on his head.

"Lawson, dear, I'm sorry. I just can't talk for a while. Why don't you curl up in the back and take a little nap?"

He pretended to do that, lying on his back the whole way to Richmond, staring at the vacant light above him as though it were a television screen that might come on with something important at any moment. Nothing came.

13

During the first week Bailey did not want to move. He wanted only absolute stillness, and the people who attended him, the motions of their care, were hateful. He saw their shadows through half-closed eyes. The pain was not sharp or wringing but incessant, as though his brain had turned into one large nerve against which the bones of his skull were gradually collapsing. He could even hear the pain. It was the sound of the gunshot extended so that it never died. Behind that noise voices only scraped, and he hated to see anyone come into the room for fear that they would speak, and in trying to listen to them he would only have to hear the blast more closely.

But that began to pass, and one morning he woke to find that he had been sleeping all night, and that except for a slight ringing in his ears and throbbing on one side of his head as though he had just rammed it hard on the corner of a piece of furniture, he could open his eyes again to the world around him. He lay very still and watched the curtains sag and flutter in the window. He knew that very soon he would even have to think. But for the moment he contented himself with the lessening of pain, sorry to hear people rising because he knew they would be in to see him. Watching the curtain seemed more than enough, and intensely uncomplicated.

Esther opened the door very carefully, shut it partway, and tiptoed to the window without looking at him.

"It's all right," he said gingerly, afraid the sound of his voice, which he had not consciously used for so long, might hurt. It was only a little distant, as though some cotton were in one ear. Esther started and turned, her eyes wide. "I'm all right now, Esther. You needn't tiptoe."

She put one hand to her throat. "You scared me." Then she smiled. "You are, aren't you?" and she stooped over him to touch his forehead very lightly with one hand. Brody put his head in the door.

"He's fine, look, he's just fine," she said and Brody came all the way in.

"Hello, Brody," and Bailey knew he was showing off, but everything felt very new to him, as though he had learned all over again how to speak.

Brody stood grinning at the foot of the bed, one beefy hand gripping the bedpost. "Welcome back."

Later that day he asked Esther where Jacqueline and Lawson were. He could tell she wanted to put that question away for a while, but he insisted. She told him everything and he took it all very quietly. He knew he must have thought it through already in the back of his mind. When she had finished he simply said, "Thank you." He was not sure whether he could make sense out of it all. Everything leading up to his putting that gun hastily to his head was remote, as though belonging to someone else. He was still too tired to think anyway and spent the day dozing and waking, listening to the breeze sagging the screen in, the distant growling of a tractor. Esther came in to turn the lights out that evening.

"You'll call them, won't you? To say I'm all right."

She paused with one hand on the switch and did not look at him directly. "She called every day for a while."

The lights went out.

The next day he tried to get up but was dizzy, and standing made him feel as though he were pressing his head against a wall. But by doing it more gradually and insisting that he be allowed to get up and walk around his room when he felt up to it, he was able to move freely about the house in four days. He found out he was deaf in one ear. He had a few talks with Brody, although his brother left little of the talking to him, and he was told more fully how matters stood. Brody talked mostly about Jacqueline and moved back and forth between indignation and puzzlement. Esther was more understanding, tried to tell him how a woman felt about all this. "You wait, Bailey dear, and don't fret. She'll come around after a bit." But Esther did not excuse him for what he had done. She let him know that as a woman she was angry and understood how hurt she would be if Brody did such a thing. But after all, it was only a lapse, and Jacqueline would see it after she was alone for a while. "Brody was right, you know," she said, "although I must admit I didn't see it that way myself at the time. But you've made your mistake and learned your lesson. It's certainly not a thing to break up sixteen happy years of a marriage." Her anger seemed especially reserved for Nora and more than once she called her "that cheap slut."

Bailey let them talk. Sometimes he wished both ears had been deafened, but he didn't have to answer much. After a while they did not seem to want to talk about it. He knew that in the back of their minds were larger questions about his attempted suicide, but they would never touch on that unless he did. They watched him carefully.

But he too was afraid to look at it. "Killed himself." He could hardly believe that he had almost done that. At first he was ashamed. But finally that did not bother him so much, the action itself seemed simple, as if he had done something not reprehensible, but foolish. Before long he began taking short walks in the evening. He would go somewhere in the fields and sit where he could see as far as possible, down the gullies to the woods, over the treetops to the blue ridges beyond. He might have lost just this—the ability to walk out on an evening and watch the sun fall and feel the long grass brush in the wind against his bare arms. When he thought of himself he knew he did not have big things to do, and nothing great would have been blown away with the bits of his brain scattered in the yard, but he would have lost his chance to feel all this. He could not tell that to Brody and Esther, could hardly explain it to himself. He almost thought his feelings were too sentimental, but then he realized they were merely too simple to be expressed.

Soon there was little pain, only an irritation from his hair growing back in around the scar and the heat of having his head wrapped so tightly. One afternoon he went to the barn. With almost a detached curiosity he walked from one end to the other, saw the gun where it had been replaced on its peg, touched it with his fingers, and then walked empty-handed to the crib and fence where he remembered standing. There was no mark, and he could not recall exactly where he had stood. The cows were in the near field, a buzzard looping off toward the ridge. He might have died here. But he almost laughed to think how typical it was of him to be so careless and remembered clearly his state of mind then as though watching a film. He played it backward, over the meetings with Nora, walks in the fields, restless nights, the wedding, and even the drive from Richmond. Then in a rush he went forward again. In all of it he found no one that he could now call himself. He looked at his hand, the one that had pulled the trigger. Had he really killed himself after all? For a moment the uncanny idea took him that someone else might have slipped into his body at the moment he passed out, a spirit waiting by the corncrib. He closed his eyes, dizzied. No, only some part of him had been sent flying like the scattering birds of his dreams. But who was he now?

He turned and walked down the red, clay-rutted drive to the lake. There, because the sun was hot in the late July afternoon, he found a beech-tree and sat with his back to the trunk, looking at the water. "Bailey Wright," he said. Even that was not true. He was stripped back to a part of himself that had no name, no history, a container, waiting again to be filled. The water glinted and blinked at him. He closed his eyes. The tree ridged against him. His head hummed and he thought of the tree's humming beyond the bark, flowing, the roots under him sucking at the layered earth, like his own cells piled into his skin, his own bones, sinewed and moving branches. He wondered as he walked home whether this was the way a baby felt when it was born, all surfaces newly cast out. Or was it like being very deeply asleep? The road dipped down to the old orange sun and the glinting windows of the house. If he had lost something when that blast surged through his head, its empty place was being filled. The sun rushed down and the hills rose over it like waves. He had never felt so peaceful.

He wanted that feeling to stay forever. But after a few days it passed. From time to time he found it again, but only in flashes. Finally he thought the wound might be affecting his mind queerly, and once, worried that he had been injured more than they had told him, he consulted the doctor. But he told Bailey not to worry.

He was restless at times and knew he would have to go soon. Once at night he came downstairs to walk about the lower floor, from room to room. The moon was out, a perfect round through the living room windows. He went into the darkened hall to reach the porch, but at the door he paused. Only the screen was between him and the bright patterns. He put his hand on its mesh and closed his eyes, imagining the old footsteps in their obstinate tread, the silence, the breaking out of hooves, and he thrust the door open to step out into the moonlight and the damp night air. Small clouds were passing high. He put one hand on the pillar near him and listened to the sound of riding, riding over the field and driveway, down to the woods that stood like a dark castle wall. "Good night, you old fool," and he closed his eyes again to let the hoofbeats die away into his own pulse and easy breathing.

He began to think often of Jacqueline and Lawson. But Jacqueline was always very young, as he had first known her, when she wore her hair so short, and in those long, willowy dresses that made her seem frail. She would smile and turn, and sometimes he had a vision of them together, he was not sure where, but they were strolling on a path of white pebbles and she would laugh as though he had been teasing her. Lawson was much younger too, maybe three or four years old, and he would run to Bailey from a distance, his arms out, laughing so hard that he was almost stumbling over his own feet, falling the last few steps into Bailey's hands, and he would lift him high, squealing and kicking, Jacqueline's voice somewhere saying, "Oh, Bailey, be careful." Where were they? Alone in his room in the early morning he sat by the window and wept.

Late that day he packed his suitcases and carried them to the top of the stairs. It was almost dinnertime. He could hear Esther and Brody talking quietly to each other on the porch. They would call him soon to come down and have a drink. Brody saw him first. "What's up?" he said as Bailey went out onto the porch. He was dressed in his suit and tie and carried his raincoat over one arm.

"I guess I'll be going now, Brody. Don't bother with anything. I'll call the taxi. There's a bus at six-thirty back to Richmond."

Esther stood. "Oh, no. You can't go now. Why, you're in no condition . . ."

"Esther, you know and I know that I'm well enough now."

"Back to Richmond?" Brody said. "But how? Where? You

know Jacqueline won't want to see . . . I mean, unless you've called her or something."

"No. I haven't called. I won't go home right away. I'll stay in a hotel and then we'll see."

"But why?" and Esther came up to put her hand on his arm.

He did not have to answer her. Even she knew it was a silly question, and they could see he was determined. Brody insisted that he drive him into town, and Bailey was very glad that the bus was on time and waiting. He kissed Esther and shook Brody's hand. His brother hugged him once, almost furtively, and then they turned to walk slowly back to the parking lot. The bus pulled out before he had found a seat. Past the new bank, the ruins of the old water tower, the big bridge over Buffalo Creek, the bus whined and lurched. For a moment he was very sad. He knew he would never be back.

He registered at a hotel downtown. It was late, and he was not hungry, so he stayed in his room. He thought of calling but decided against it. They would probably be in bed by now, and what could he say to her on a telephone anyway? He was afraid of not finding them there. He had to believe they were in the house he knew so well, Lawson probably already asleep, Jacqueline reading late or if she was not upstairs, sitting on the patio to cool off before going to bed. After trying the television for a while, he turned out the lights and lay on his back. His head still hurt if he put any weight on it so he carefully bunched the pillows, then lay there not trying to sleep or caring if he watched the night pass. He dozed from time to time but woke often to the room slatted with light by a neon advertisement somewhere outside that shifted gradually from red, to blue, to green, to red.

14

In Richmond Lawson found himself even more lonely than in the country. Many of his friends were away on vacation and those who had remained he avoided anyway. He willed his loneliness with bitterness, stubbornly. His father was not there, not even to be mentioned as he discovered once at dinner, and he avoided his mother as much as possible, even though he could tell at times that hurt her.

Sometimes, when he could not read and even the television had nothing he wanted to watch, he thought about his father. But he never saw him very clearly. What he saw again and again was a man, dressed like his father and with his back to him, trying to shoot himself, and he had a large dueling pistol in his hand. He kept raising it to his head, and when it almost touched him, he would let it drop as though it were too heavy and his arm too weak. Lawson was certain that one of the reasons his father had shot himself was because Bailey had seen him looking into the cabin, and Lawson was ashamed that he had told on his father. Again and again he persuaded himself he had not meant to and did not know why he had. If only he had kept his mouth shut.

His mother was very different now, as though what he had told her hurt so badly that she had died and someone else had taken her place. If he had not told, they might all still be in the country and he would be where he could talk to his father. He wanted to do that very badly sometimes, just to ask his father if he had seen him, why didn't he chase him or yell? Above all he was angry that he had joined sides with his Uncle Brody. What Brody said had turned out to be true and he did not want to be on Brody's side. He decided he hated him and always would. But what side was he really on? He had joined Brody and Brody was a Wright, but his mother had taken him away and said they would never see the Wrights again, and she was an Ambler. Why did he have to choose like that?

Sometimes he also wanted to yell at his father, who had tried to kill himself. That was a terrible thing to do. Once they had read *Julius Caesar* in class and they had talked about suicide. The teacher said it was very cowardly. And what his father had done to his mother was a bad thing, so bad that they could not love each other anymore. That made his father a coward and very unfair. The more he thought about it, the more he decided he did not really want to see his father ever again either. His father, after all, was in his own way as bad as Brody. That left him with his mother, in Richmond, and living like this for a long time to come. She wanted him to be nice to her and to talk with her about all these things that he was thinking, but he was angry at her too. She had taken him away from his father, probably forever. In all this muddle he could not see the inconsistencies, and try as he would to ignore them, his thoughts circled him back and forth through an endless tangle, and at night what he had avoided by day made him restless in strange, confused dreams that seemed to have nothing to do with anything he had ever seen or known.

When he decided to run away, he thought first of going to Bonnie. But that was too close to the farm again, and what could she do but turn him over to Esther and Brody? Once she called, but his mother was there and talked to her for a long time, and when he was given the phone, she did not leave the room, so he could not say anything he wanted to. And anyway, talking didn't help. She asked him some questions, and finally there was a long silence in which he heard nothing but waves and cracklings.

"Lawson, I'm going to come visit in a week or so. I want to see you."

He wanted to say yes, yes, but something restrained him.

"OK."

"Let me talk to your mother again."

He handed the phone back to her and left the room.

Finally Lawson went to visit Edward. He was in Tucker's again, and Lawson knew his way through the iron gates with the rampant gold lions, up the pebbled path across the lawn where some of the patients wandered slowly with white-aproned attendants, or a family clustered around someone, listening carefully to every word. He passed a croquet game where two men were standing over a wicket, staring blankly at their mallets as if they had forgotten what they were for. Just as he had expected, Uncle Edward was sitting on the porch, hands folded in his lap and staring off toward the ginkgo tree.

"Hello, Uncle Edward."

He frowned, as if a very distant voice had come out of the tree itself.

"It's me, Lawson."

The face turned, the wide eyes still focused beyond Lawson's head, and then they snapped into place.

"Oh, Lawson. Where did you come from?"

"I walked."

Suddenly Edward leaned forward and touched Lawson's arm, and then he smiled.

"Sorry. I just have to check, you know. Sometimes I get to talking and find out later there's no one there."

"I'm here," Lawson said simply, and Edward nodded.

The click of the croquet balls came up to them, and on the far end of the porch someone was laughing feverishly, as if he could not stop but wanted to.

"Uncle Edward," Lawson said suddenly, "have you ever tried to kill yourself?"

Edward did not seem annoyed by the question. He only stared at Lawson.

"Perhaps."

"I really want to know. I want to know why you would."

Edward frowned as if trying to remember.

"Well, it was a long time ago. I'm not sure I could say I really wanted to die. I was just trying to kill my self."

Lawson sat on the end of the chaise longue nearby. "How can that be? I mean if you kill yourself, you're dead."

"Yes, but sometimes you just want to be different, to kill everything about yourself you can't live with, but you're too angry at all that to really think you, yourself, are going to die."

Lawson tried to understand, but could only see his father's bandaged head, the body under its sheets.

"My dad tried, you know."

"I know." Edward put out his hand again, the fingers heavy and immobile. "That's too bad. Is he all right?"

"I guess so."

"I thought I knew what I wanted then," Edward said vaguely. "I thought I wouldn't have it and that I didn't want to be around without it. I'm not sure even what it was, now," and he looked at the hand, palm up in his lap, as if someone had left it there.

Lawson stood up.

"I'm going to run away, Uncle Edward."

"Oh? Where to?"

Lawson sat down again.

"I don't know."

Edward put his hand on Lawson's knee. "Well, you should plan that out a little. I ran away once, from here, about five years ago. I hadn't thought about it too carefully and they caught me down at the park. By that time I'd figured out I didn't really want to go anyplace else much."

"I'll just get on a bus. I have enough money, and when my ticket runs out, I'll get off."

Edward shook his head. "There are places I'd rather not get off a bus."

Suddenly Lawson was angry. "Well, why not? Nothing's as bad as here."

They didn't say anything for a while. The man at the other end of the porch had stopped laughing but now he was chanting in a shrill voice, "Cra-zy, cra-zy," and clapping his hands on the first syllable.

"Will you run away with me?" Lawson had not known he would say that, but suddenly he thought it would be good to have some company.

Edward looked at him. The hazel eyes, very soft and dilated, seemed to be all of his face as Lawson stared at them. But the man slowly shook his head, smiling.

"I have, Lawson," he said quietly. "I already have."

Lawson did not understand. All he knew was that something so sweet and mild and loving was in the man's face that he wanted to cry. Instead he turned his back and stared down over the lawn toward the birdbath, but he held onto his uncle's hand as if it were the only thing that prevented him from floating off into the ragged blue sky.

A nurse came soon. Visiting hours were over. He said goodbye, and Edward whispered, "Don't go too far away," and then Lawson walked home. He wasn't ready to run away yet, he decided.

He awoke that night from a dream to find himself sitting straight up in bed. The moon was shining so brightly that it hurt his eyes. There had been a stone castle wall behind him, a moat ahead, and he was riding out, precariously seated on a horse without reins. Across the river a bright, heart-shaped light was flashing and wheeling like a meteor falling away from him into the woods. The images left him quickly and what remained was only an uneasy sense that he might fall at any moment, which would be shameful because somewhere behind him a person who mattered was watching, probably Bonnie, although he could not see her clearly when he turned, only a dim figure on a high parapet. Then he saw the oblong window of his room, the gum tree tinseled by the light, and suddenly a mockingbird tried out a long and twisting call. He rubbed his eyes, wondering if he had been talking because he remembered the sound of voices. The mockingbird paused and then began again.

Lawson went to the window. Below he could see the garden and the patio. It had to be very late because no light shone out from the floor below and there was no sound of traffic. For the first time since he had come back he remembered that he had buried something in the garden before he left, and that he had intended to dig it up when he returned. What was it? He went to the bedroom door. Nothing seemed to move in the house. The stairs creaked a little as he went down, but by staying close to the wall he made less noise. The pen that Fanny had given him. That was it. He felt sure of the spot he had buried it in. He was curious to see what weeks of lying in the earth had done to it.

The pebbles were smooth and he stepped lightly. When he reached the far edge of the fountain, he kneeled where the myrtle had grown over the edge of the path and began digging at the place with his hands. The earth was still damp from being watered that morning, and he dug down as far as he knew he needed to go. The pen was not there. He looked over his shoulder at the fountain and by sighting it against the house, he decided he was too far to the right. He dug again. Nothing. He joined the two holes he had made by a trench, then crumbled up the dirt he had piled to see if it could be there. The myrtle obscured the bottom of the hole, but everywhere else the light shone out as though lying behind the objects it touched. He paused and sat back on his heels. He had begun to sweat. The mockingbird, rustling around from time to time in the branches of the gum tree, was not disturbed by him and sang incessantly.

Lawson began to have an eery, half-waking feeling and wondered if someone had dug there in his absence. What would anyone want with an old ball-point pen that did not work? He began to dig frantically all along the border of the path until he knew he had gone too far and then he went back and started in the opposite direction.

"Lawson?"

He held perfectly still. The bird stopped singing. The sound of a voice, even though he knew immediately that it was his mother's, frightened him. He heard her walking to him over the path and he stood. Her nightgown was a pliant film of aluminum, and her hair a dark seam down one side of her face.

"Lawson Wright. What in the world?"

She reached to touch him and he pulled back, standing on the myrtle.

"Child, what is the matter? Are you awake?"

"I buried it. It's not here. Who's been digging?"

"You're not awake. You're sleepwalking aren't you?" and she said, "Lawson," loudly and firmly.

"I'm awake," and he decided not to tell her about it.

"Then what are you doing here?"

He saw that his mother, although trying to sound angry, was the one who was upset now.

"I was just playing. I couldn't sleep."

"You come in this house at once," and she held out her hand.

He did not take it, but walked by her to the house. When they were both inside she turned on the kitchen light, and they stood there, blinking and narrow-eyed.

"Lawson, look at your hands and your pajamas. They're filthy."

He was caked with dirt to his elbows, the knees of his pajamas stained black.

"Come here."

She turned him by the shoulder and guided him to the kitchen sink. Then she took his hands and began washing them as though he were a child again. Her hair, hanging undone, brushed against his face as she stood over him.

"Oh, Lord, Lord," she muttered. "What is happening? I wake in the middle of the night and find my son digging in the garden, and Edward has gone all to pieces again, and . . ." but she paused as though to follow out her own train of thought in her mind. "Why? Lawson, what were you doing?"

Her hand was under his chin and she turned his face to her. He wanted for a moment to explain it all. Above all he just wanted to clasp himself to her and feel her arms around his back. But even as he looked he saw how her face had changed in the past weeks, a leanness from her loss of weight, the strange dark half-moons of shadow under her eyes.

"Nothing. I told you."

"Lawson, Lawson, what are you doing to me?" and her eyes were filling with tears.

"I should have died. I should have. When my bike got smashed. I wish I'd died then."

He wrenched away from her to run to the kitchen door. Then he turned.

"I hate you, I hate both of you," and he ran upstairs to his room, afraid she would catch him or touch him because he knew that if she did he would not be able to keep himself back any longer.

She came to his door after a while and opened it. He lay on his back in bed.

"Lawson?"

"Yes."

"I understand. I do. Can we talk about all this tomorrow? I won't come in now if you'd rather I didn't."

"Don't."

"All right." For a while she did not move. "We will talk tomorrow, won't we?"

"I guess," and then he heard the door snap softly shut.

Lawson did not want to talk to her and he knew he should not lie, but he had to. He sat up. The mockingbird was not singing now, but chirped from time to time and made noises as though beating its wings against the leaves.

"I won't be a Wright *or* an Ambler," he whispered firmly to himself and said it over and over until the moonlight faded and the sky behind was growing gray with a different kind of light.

15

Bailey was prepared to stay in the hotel for some time and expected that Jacqueline might even refuse to see him at first, so when it took him a week of phoning every day to get her permission to visit, he was not angry, but kept calling patiently. The room was sufficient, the hotel, although not the best, at least inexpensive and clean, and he even began reading the newspaper ads for apartments.

He paid the cab and stood for a moment looking up at the front windows, wondering if anyone had seen him, but they were empty. To stand on the sidewalk and think of the familiar house as his but closed to him was strange, and he had to walk down the block to wait a while for his nerve to come back to him. He had a key but knew he should not use it.

He was about to ring again when the door opened. She stood for a minute as though not recognizing him, then glanced at his bandages and away.

"Well," she said.

"Hello, Jacqueline."

His voice sounded unnatural even to him, but she seemed to find strength in that awkwardness and looked him directly in the eyes.

"May I come in?"

"All right."

"I wanted to talk a moment."

"I'm not sure it will help. But come on."

As they walked into the living room she kept well away from him, as if afraid that they might touch by accident. She asked him how he was and they went to the patio, both saying it would be nice to sit outside. For a while their conversation was very broken. He told her about what the doctor said, about leaving Esther and Brody, and as he talked he became more and more desperate at the irrelevance of what he was saying and at the tightness of her lips as she sat in the iron filigree chair, her arms clasped to her.

"Then you're not going to see a psychiatrist or anything?"

"No. I don't think I need to."

They were silent, and he saw he would have to begin it himself. How fiercely and proudly she sat there, not exactly what he had expected. At least he had supposed she would be emotional, one way or the other.

"And Lawson? How is Lawson?"

"He's upset. Shouldn't he be?"

"Where is he?"

"He's at the movies. I'm not sure I want you to see him."

He had not counted on her calm, this nearly hieratic pose like an Egyptian statuette, and the way she spoke so firmly when in other days she would have trembled on the verge of tears. In all his imaginings of what he would do or say he had seen her as the person he had known, although turned against him. Now he was at a loss how to begin.

"Don't we need to talk?"

"I suppose."

He put a hand to his lips and then sat back.

"Except I don't know where to begin, or how. I feel so self-conscious."

She glanced at him and smiled thinly.

"I suppose I can't help enjoying making you a little uncomfortable. It did hurt, you know," and she seemed more herself to him then.

He began talking. She started to speak, but he told her to let him say some things first, and she did. He could not tell if she was really listening, but after a while he accepted her pose, hands folded in her lap, face turned to the garden wall and long legs stretched out to cross thinly at her ankles. He tried to explain what he understood, did not say he was sorry, knowing how cheap that would sound, but described it all as best he could, and he found that as he went it became easier, he talked more vehemently until he was leaning forward in his chair, gesturing with his hands. Still she never looked at him. He tried to explain how it was for him now, faltered, and stopped. They were both quiet again. He leaned back in his chair, very tired.

"I'm trying to say I love you."

She looked at him, then down at her lap. "Bailey, you needn't have said that. Or anything, really. I think I know most of what you said. Or I've guessed at it in the past weeks."

"Then you forgive me?" and he was immediately sorry he had said that.

"No. Not yet. I just said I understand. I didn't say I accepted it."

He nodded.

"And forgiving means you kind of accept it all, doesn't it? Well, I don't yet," and her voice was bitter now. "I know I'm not the first woman who's had an unfaithful husband, and I know it was only a moment in all our lives, although believe me for a while I suspected it was going on more than I thought. Long before."

"It wasn't," he said quickly. "I may have thought of it, but it wasn't."

"I'll believe you. In my mind I can imagine anything, but when I see you like this, I know it couldn't have happened before. You wouldn't have been able to keep it from me."

She said that as though it were a weakness in him, and he almost felt offended.

"But do you love me?"

She walked to the edge of the patio where she stood with her back to him.

"I don't know. I want to think about a lot of things."

Her anger or jealousy he could have stood. But this was new and strange, almost indifference, certainly distant.

"What does that mean?"

"I need time. Time to myself. Maybe I've needed that anyway and never knew it. Time apart from you. I don't think about that girl anymore. I think about how I let you mean too much to me, more than another person should to anyone."

"I can't live very well without you and Lawson."

"I didn't say it was the end. I just said I need some time alone."

He felt helpless. Always in the past his words and actions had an immediate effect on her. He saw a long, neutral separation, her being without him and not needing him and she might decide not to return. Perhaps there would even be other men. Above all he saw that nothing would be the same again no matter what happened, that the thing they had called love and their marriage was altered and unknown, and that frightened him.

"Jacqueline." He stood.

"No. I mean it."

She turned, her hands clasped to her elbows, so self-enclosed that touching her or trying other words would be useless.

"All right. But I'm warning you, I won't disappear. If I have to, I'll woo you until I win you again."

She smiled, almost relaxed. "That doesn't sound too bad. Although I warn you also that I won't be as easy a mark as last time."

But he could not find the humor to carry on in that vein, so they turned awkwardly back into the house. At the door, which she opened for him as though he were a guest, she let him pause.

"Is there anything you want to pick up?"

"No. I think I've got everything I need for now. And Lawson, you'll let me know how things go with him?"

"You can call, if you like."

"I will. I want to see him as soon as I can."

He started out, but turned. She was leaning against the door now, her face sadder than he had seen it since he came in. He stepped toward her but she put up a hand, palm outward.

"No."

He nodded, turned away, and looked up from the street to see the door close behind him. As he walked slowly downtown again Bailey tried to see things from her point of view. Could he have been too protective, too eager to keep her from all those irritations and petty hurts, in the process making their relationship too narrow and confined? She had been willing to have it that way. But what if he had "protected" her for his sake also—to avoid her anger and depressions, to somehow keep her to himself, safe and preoccupied with his own being. He had taken very few risks with her. For years she had been so dependent on him, which he had thought he dreaded because sometimes her clinging, the way she wanted him to tell her everything on his mind, made him nervously back off, making some space lest he be absorbed, dragged down. Now he realized how lonely it was without her concern. Already she seemed so different. Back in his room, he knew he had lost something forever.

He was very tired and without eating went to bed early in the evening. Immediately he fell asleep and began dreaming. He was dead. But somehow he had been allowed to rise and hover invisibly above his grave as each one of his friends and family came to look down on the scarred, black lid of his coffin, some to drop a handful of earth, others just to stand there. He had never seen the place before, cypresses bent slightly in a wind that did not reach down to him, and winged figures of marble nearby. Even though they did not speak, he could hear their thoughts, and each one of them, Jacqueline, Lawson (strangely older, in a dark suit with polished shoes), even Nora, had one whispered phrase like a litany: "Why did he use me?" Each time he heard it he winced and wanted to reach out to touch them, but his hands passed over their faces and arms like mist. What hurt him most of all was that they did not ask the question in anger or bitterness, but as if puzzled and in pain.

He rolled uneasily in bed, half woke and found himself in a dark hallway. Ahead was a bright crack of light, so bright it seared his eyes, and as he approached, he had to look at its reflection on the floor, hand on his brow. Finally he stood there peering in, and they were all inside, seated around a large table where food and fruits were jumbled ripely, even Nora and Esther and Brody and Bonnie, and they were laughing, eating, touching each other. The light seemed to pulse out of the center of the table and when he tried to stare at it he knew he would go blind if he did for long, so he looked at the people instead. Jacqueline saw him, and she smiled shyly, as she sometimes did when she stood naked before him in the daytime. "Come in. Please. We've been waiting." They all turned. Brody said, "Here he is," and Lawson ran over to take him by the hand. He loved them, and as he came toward the table the light from its shimmering center went so deep into his eyes that his head was like the room, with no dark corners in it, and his arms seemed to be able to touch all of them at once, and he wept.

The telephone was ringing. He clutched it in confusion. Jacqueline's voice.

"Bailey, please come over. Now."

"Why?"

"Lawson. He's locked in his room. He won't come out."

Bailey started to laugh, thought better of it, and asked instead, "How long?"

"Just come, will you? He says he's going to shoot himself."

He told her not to worry, he was on his way, and then hung up. But he ran down the stairs rather than wait for the elevator.

16

Lawson packed his suitcase, and two hours later he unpacked it. Where could he go? He carried the empty bag back to the cellar. There was no one to go to. He would only be found somewhere by the police and brought back, like three years ago when he did not get his toboggan for Christmas and tried to run off to Canada. He was stuck.

He knew where his father's pistol was and he had been taught how to load it when they went to target practice. Without any clear intent, he had taken it from the closet shelf that morning, found the shells in the garage, and hidden both behind a pile of games in his bookshelf. He thought that if he did not possess it, his mother might lock it away, and that did not seem right. All day he felt slightly exhilarated, as though he owned a secret power no one else could touch. That night he hardly ate at all and was eager to go to his room early so that he could have his door securely closed and then take out the gun to hold and finger it.

But as he started up the stairs, his mother called to him.

"I want to talk to you, Lawson."

He did not answer so she came to the landing below.

"I don't want to." He clutched the banister, unwilling to turn fully to her.

"I know that. But we have to."

"No, we don't. I don't if I don't want to."

"Lawson. You only make me worry more when you talk like that."

"I'm not just talking. I mean it."

He could hear her take a few steps up, then pause.

"I saw your father today."

"Where?"

"Here. This afternoon. He came to talk to me."

"You knew he was coming?"

"No."

"It was a secret."

"Secret?"

"From me."

"No, he just came."

But Lawson did not trust her.

"Why do you want to see him at all? I thought you hated him?"

"He's your father, Lawson. We're married still."

She was speaking gently, yet her words seemed to slap him. His throat clenched.

"He's not my father. Not anymore," and turning, he looked down for the first time into her face, half-hooded by the shadows, but he could see her eyes distinctly. "And you're not my mother."

"Lawson," and she was moving toward him as though floating up out of a deep well, her eyes fixed on him.

"No. Don't come near me."

She stopped. He began to back up the rest of the stairs.

"Leave me alone," and he leaped up the last steps, slammed

the door to his bedroom behind him, and twisted the key. In a moment he had the gun, loaded it, and then, seeing what he had done, stood by the window, holding it in both his hands because he was trembling so violently. When she knocked he closed his eyes.

"Lawson. Please. You frighten me."

There was a silence, how long he could not measure. He swallowed and his throat burned back at him.

"Go away. I'm going to shoot myself."

"Lawson . . ."

"I've got the gun," and he heard his voice almost laughing, jubilant. "I've got the gun. Leave me alone."

He even had his finger on the trigger and held it properly at last. But her silence made him pause. In a few minutes he realized that she had left. He walked to the door, leaned his head against it, and held his breath. After a while he thought he could hear her voice. Probably phoning. Who? The police. An ambulance. Suddenly it was all very real. He could do it. He looked at the gun again. She might be calling his father. He sat on the edge of the bed as though his knees had slipped out of joint. He had some time, anyway. The gun was very heavy and he put it on the bed beside him, the barrel carefully pointed toward the window.

He tried to think, but couldn't. It was as though he had been told that he must go to his room, memorize everything in it, and then report back for a test. He could only grasp at the surface, his eyes wandering from bookshelf, to window, to the chairs, the television set, the door to the bathroom, and yet when he had moved that far he could not remember what he had just seen and he had to go back to the beginning again. Sometime later he heard the front door slam. Then footsteps along the corridor. He turned his head as though he had been struck by the voice. His father's voice.

"Can you hear me, son? Let me in."

"No." He stared at the doorknob, watched it turn one way and then the other.

"Lawson."

"No." He stood. "I can't. I won't."

"You will. I'm here, Lawson. Open the door."

"Here? You've come home?"

There was a silence.

"I am here now."

"Then you're playing a game with me, aren't you? You only want to take the gun away."

Lawson reached down and picked it up, but the voice would not let him alone.

"It is no game," his father said so quietly that Lawson had to lean toward the door. "I won't lie to you, that's all. I'm here to see you. We need to talk."

"What do you want?"

Lawson opened his mouth, found no words, and touched the door with his flattened palm.

"Where's Mother?"

"She's here too."

"Do you love her?"

"Yes," came the voice quickly and firmly again.

Lawson looked at the window, the bureau, the rumpled bed.

"I'm going to unlock the door. But don't come in until I tell you."

"I won't."

"Promise?"

"Yes."

He turned the key and then walked around the end of the bed so that it stood between himself and the door.

"All right. You can come in."

The door opened. His father was standing there. Again the bandage on his head shocked Lawson, and the pale, thin face made his father seem so much younger. Back, whirling in a corner of his mind was a memory of him like that, somewhere long ago, and there was a tree in bloom nearby bleaching the air, someone calling a name distinctly, rain beginning to fall, and yet the birds were rising like flecks of gold away from the darkening lawn.

"Hello, son."

He could see his mother dimly behind in the dark corridor.

"I'm coming in," and he did.

"Stop. There."

He was across the threshold looking at the gun and the shaking hand that held it.

"Bailey," Jacqueline said, but he only raised his hand.

"We'll be all right. I'm going to shut the door for a few minutes now."

"Why?" Lawson said.

"Because we need to talk, alone," and suddenly they were in the room together with the door closed.

"What are you doing? Let me out."

"Give me the gun." Bailey reached out with one hand, almost touching Lawson's arm.

"I saw you there," and Lawson raised the gun as if to point at the cabin wall. "I saw you and her naked."

"I know."

"Well, why didn't you yell, then? Why didn't you chase me?"

"I didn't see *you*."

"I told them."

"Yes. You had to. That was right."

Lawson frowned. "Why? You tried to kill yourself. Why?"

Bailey's eyes followed the gun as Lawson motioned with it.

"Yes. I did."

"I don't understand." Knowing he was losing by the way his voice trembled and his vision began to blur, he became angry with himself, even more so when he realized he could never really use the gun.

"Don't try. Not now. When I can understand it myself a little better, I promise to tell you. But you don't need to know everything now."

"But I want to. I want to know," and he threw the gun on the bed and heard the springs give to it. For a moment he could not move. The gun landed as if some heavy part of him had been torn away and dropped, and it lay there between them, hard and evil in its shape. Lawson tried to see his father clearly, his bandages gleaming like a white hood, the straight and simple figure, and stumbling against the side of the bed he leaped to the hands that took him. He did not cry, and Bailey held him quietly.

After a while they sat down on the window seat where they could see the street below. They did not say much. Bailey talked a little about leaving the country and how he had missed them there. Then he called out, "You can come in now, Jacqueline."

For a few minutes she stood beside them. Lawson could tell they were looking at each other, but he did not want to see.

"Will you stay?" he asked his father finally.

He shook his head. "Not yet, Lawson."

"Why?"

"Your mother and I have to work this out. In our own time. You have to be patient."

"But you will?"

Then both of them looked at Jacqueline. She did not give any sign that Lawson could see, but Bailey said, "We will."

When his father left an hour later they all stood at the door, a little awkwardly, as though each one of them had something more to say but could not remember what.

"I'll see you tomorrow evening," Bailey said to him, and when he put his hand on Lawson's shoulder, a whole day seemed like a long time to wait. But he remembered also that tomorrow Bonnie would be coming, and suddenly he thought there would be a great deal to talk about.

A bus passed rattling and almost empty, a breeze whirled in around them, and somewhere on the second floor a door slammed with a muffled crack.

"Yes," Lawson said tentatively, and then as though leaping into the word, "yes."